BASIC BLACK WITH PEARLS

HELEN WEINZWEIG

Afterword by
SARAH WEINMAN

NEW YORK REVIEW BOOKS

New York

THIS IS A NEW YORK REVIEW BOOK
PUBLISHED BY THE NEW YORK REVIEW OF BOOKS
435 Hudson Street, New York, NY 10014
www.nyrb.com

First published in Canada in 1980 by House of Anansi Press

Library of Congress Cataloging-in-Publication Data
Names: Weinzweig, Helen, 1915– author. | Weinman, Sarah, author of afterword.
Title: Basic black with pearls / by Helen Weinzweig ; afterword by Sarah Weinman.
Description: New York : New York Review Books, [2018] | Series: New York Review
  Books Classics
Identifiers: LCCN 2017045337 | ISBN 9781681372167 (paperback) | ISBN
  9781681372174 (epub)
Subjects: | BISAC: FICTION / Contemporary Women. | FICTION / Psychological.
Classification: LCC PR9199.3.W4 B3 2018 | DDC 823/.912—dc23
LC record available at https://lccn.loc.gov/2017045337

ISBN 978-1-68137-216-7
Available as an electronic book; ISBN 978-1-68137-217-4

Printed in the United States of America on acid-free paper.
10 9 8 7 6 5 4 3 2 1

I asked him to take off his mask, but this is all I have, he replied.
Take it off I commanded. He did so. It's no use I still cannot recognize
you — put the mask back on — there that's better now that I know
I don't know you we can talk more easily.
Ann Quin, *Passages*

NIGHT COMES AS a surprise in the tropics. There is no twilight, no preparation for the disappearance of light. One moment the eyes must be protected from a merciless sun and the next, it seems, all forms vanish into the black night. I was sleepless in Tikal. As soon as night fell the pariah dogs began their barking, which went on all through the night until the first flush of dawn, when they ceased as abruptly as they began. That morning, early, I took a tour of the ruins. I was in a group of tourists, pretending to be one of them, all the while hanging about the edge of the little band, ready, at a signal, to leave them. I listened carefully to the native guide, whose English was remarkably good. Was he my lover? I moved along with the rest, all the while alert to the possible signs memorized from the *National Geographic,* Volume 148, number 6, *The Maya.*

Coenraad and I have a code for our meetings, taking the printed word and interpreting it according to mathematical formulae. Our safety lies in the regularity inherent in the systems of pages and lines following in simple numerical sequence, such as page-two-followed-by-line-two, page-four-followed-by-line-four, or, sometimes, odd-numbers-in-sequence. These simple arrangements, together with a degree of imagination, can put the most astute agent off the track. No one is prepared for the obvious. The code also permits me to check out whether I am in the right place on the right day; and also whether circumstances are propitious for our rendezvous. To cite an example: in Washington two years ago in the Mayfair Hotel I was handed Volume 144, number two, of the *Geographic*. On page 246, in an article on the Common Tern, reading between lines three, five and seven, that "courting pairs weave zig-zag patterns," I deduced that I must exercise caution because of the "comintern" in the capital city, and that my lover would have to zigzag, as it were, to join me. The code works most of the time.

I observed the guide more closely. He was the same height and shape as my lover. The fact that he had brown eyes, whereas Coenraad's are a steely gray, did not discourage me. Hair, skin and eye colors are so readily altered these days, they no longer serve as clues to identity. When we reached the top of the broad stone stairway to the Temple of the Giant Jaguar the guide turned to make a head-count of his little troupe. He said that his Mayan ancestors were skilled in the science of numbers. I became alert.

To them, he added, past and future were indistinguishable.

Was this said for my benefit?

Back down in the Great Plaza the tour ended where it had begun — at the tomb of the mighty Pacal. The guide pointed to a huge stone slab in front of the sarcophagus. He said, And when the shadow of Kukulcan falls diagonally across the altar, a virgin will be ravished by the high priest. The others straggled into the cool shade of the bar. I remained behind. But he wasn't Coenraad after all: he didn't stand the way my lover stands, foursquare, with an obstinate attachment to the ground. When I see that stance of Coenraad's all fears disappear: babies don't die, cars don't collide, planes fly on course, muzak is silenced, certitude reigns. That is how I always recognize my love: the way he stands, the way I feel.

The old impossible longing in the night. I cannot bear it. Often I turn over onto my left side, since I have found that lying on my left erases the searing pictures inside my head. The left side must be the one which deals with the possible, politics of the left side where illusions vanish and facts become irrefutable. Prices were up in Tikal. I should have counted my money. But my left side failed me. All about me insects were making dry scratchy noises and I began to think of that time in Celya when we soon outwitted the cockroaches by sleeping in a hammock. After we had mastered its hazards by lying across the width, that night became one of the most satisfying nights of my life. Now I faced the realization that the message which brought me to Guatemala must have been the penultimate one and that the ultimate message was yet to come. I was tempted to turn back on my right side and not deal with the problem. Instead, I rolled on my back in the hope that this position would allow a compromise between desire and reality. It came to me that while waiting for Coenraad, the practical thing to do would be to study the handicraft of the region.

All at once the dogs became quiet, the insects stopped their scratching. They knew something was about to happen. And when the knock came on my door, I leapt and ran to answer it. A skinny boy had come for me. He was too young to be a night clerk. But his resigned dark eyes were ancient. In the tiny lobby downstairs he pointed to the telephone, its receiver on the Formica counter, and returned to his iron cot in the doorway to the street. He was sound asleep before I said *Si?* into the phone. The operators had a great deal to tell each other in excited Spanish before Coenraad and I were permitted to speak to each other.

– Listen carefully, forget the message.

– What's wrong, have they cracked our code?

– No, my superior wants it.

– Let him get his own, it took us years to perfect it.

– He's my boss, I have no choice.

– I won't give it up.

– It's out of my hands.

– What does a man in his position want with a second-hand code?

– He met a second-hand lady.

– We are not amused.

– No offence . . .

– We had it down to a science.

– I'll put in for a transfer to *The American Scholar*.

– Too parochial.

– If you're going to be fussy . . .

– No, no, I'll take anything in print.

– You will find instructions in pocket in back of seat in front of you on the next plane to Toronto.

– Toronto! I can't go back there.

– It's just another city.

– But that's where I live.

– Take it or leave it. That's my next assignment.

On the plane I examined the contents of the pocket on the back of the seat in front of me, but no matter how long and how hard I stretched my imagination, I found no hidden message in the booklet on the use of the oxygen mask; nor on the card show-ing locations of emergency exits; nor inside an empty paper bag. The magazine *En Route* in French and in English had beautiful photographs of Lake Louise and of skiers in Quebec and of per-fume bottles for duty-free purchase. I kept turning the pages until

I came across a leaflet, loose, between pages 25 and 26. Since this was the 25th of November, my hopes rose: after all, Coenraad had never failed me. It was a pamphlet, a political tract, titled "Canada First!", printed on cheap paper by the *Canada First Committee*. The opening statements were about Canada being treated like a kept woman, and the word "abdicate" was used three times on the first page. To my mind this was the message, pointing to King Edward VII and his kept women and King Edward VIII who had abdicated, and, by inference, pointing to the hotel in Toronto called the King Edward. I continued to read further, in the knowledge that Coenraad and I would disagree about nationalism, to which he is opposed. My pulse quickened when I visualized that first moment of our meeting: the shutting of a door behind him, the removal of disguise, the fierce kisses, the passionate embraces, the first quick climax.

At Malton, or any other airport for that matter, it is impossible to evoke images of Coenraad. For one thing, the air is turgid with other people's emotions; their thoughts take up all the available atmosphere. Moreover, airport routines leave me stupefied. I line up, get ticketed; line up for customs, for security inspection; I line up to sit in the lounge and wait; and if I'm lucky and there is no unexpected delay, I line up and board. At airports my senses leave me: I no longer hear muzak; faces float as if in water. For hours I read, I don't read; I eat, I can't eat; I drink tea, coffee, gin. In the air, confined and crowded, I am prepared for disaster in two languages.

Once I asked Coenraad how he stands it — the time changes, the long hours of imprisonment. It's the power, he replied, that surge of power that pulls the craft away from the ground. And as the earth tilts and the plane begins its long, strong pull upward;

and cars and houses diminish until they disappear altogether; and we soar above the clouds under a flawless sky — that power is mine. Then it is that I feel the throb of the motors; the vibrations begin at the soles of my feet, travel up the backs of my legs, up into my spine; and unless I do something to distract myself, unless I make out my expense account or concentrate on *Fortune* magazine, I am ready to attack the woman sitting beside me. I want to pump like the engines.

His confession surprised and moved me. I had never heard him speak so poetically.

Now I was lining up in the aisle to disembark. I was thanked for flying. Then began the walk along endless deserted corridors, up an escalator, another lineup.

– What is the purpose of your visit? a uniformed man at Immigration asks.

These are strange times and I must be careful. I finger the pearls at my throat, my coat is open to reveal a basic black dress. Now that I am middle-aged I have a slight advantage in these situations. I try to give off that mixture of confusion and unhappiness that will make him reluctant to detain me, for in that state I remind him of his mother.

– A holiday, I reply.

Even as he stamps my passport he is already appraising the next person in line.

A long wait for my suitcase, a lineup for customs, and finally, the lineup for the bus. The passage from one part of the world to another has been silent and unfelt. My voyage has meant nothing to anyone.

Not until we were driving along the Lakeshore did I come out of my daze. In those gray waters I had learned to swim. It is going to be difficult to remain anonymous in this city where I had scratched the name *Lola* into wet cement outside the library on

St. George Street, above the neat stamp of the contractor, *Felucci*, 1942. *Lola* (it is not my name) stays in my vision among the lines of speeding cars; she roller-skates in front of skyscrapers; she holds up street signs. I observe her in her misfit dresses and ridiculous coats. I feel sorry for the girl who (still) wanders darkening streets carrying two or three library books, shifting them now and again from left arm to right and back again. Sometimes both arms hold the books across her chest like a shield. They belong together, she and her books, and as long as she carries them, she is safe. The writers of books will become her familiars and protect her from betrayal. In the years in which I see her, she remains pale and thin; she hardly seems to grow; her breasts do not increase appreciably in size, although shortly after her thirteenth birthday she wears a brassiere to suppress her nipples. I watch her leave the wide street of grocery stores and fish markets and dry-goods shops and small factories and turn south (it is always south) where rows of narrow houses, separated only by tin drainpipes, are without lights, their doors shut fast. The doors are of solid, heavy wood, dark-stained, and fit tightly into their frames. She approaches one of these houses. The door yields to a strong push from her shoulder. All who live there are in a state of anger and pain, given to violent quarrels and helpless silences. Sometimes these people are relatives of sorts; or it is a Scottish couple, the husband working in the C.N.R. stables. The house smells of manure. It isn't an unpleasant odor. Once it is the house of a fat man who almost becomes her stepfather. Houses where there are three kitchens and one toilet and mattresses everywhere. I watch her mount dark stairs. Someone slips out of somewhere to secure the lock on the door behind her. That is the only sign that her homecoming has been noticed. And so she continues up the steps, to the second floor, or to the third floor; for two winters she is seen going down the hall to an unheated addition behind the kitchen, where her cot stands in the midst of potatoes and onions. Her mother is given to sudden attacks of hysteria and they move often. Now her mother is in a deep sleep, snoring, exhausted. Even as I watch that girl she climbs again and again, changing from child to young woman, up on a cot, a sofa, a bed. No one has spoken her name. No one has said goodnight.

The first few minutes in a hotel are always the same. The order of procedure is this: I approach the desk and fill out a little card with the (false) name on my passport. Except when I am in New York, I give as my domicile the address of the United Nations. On the line provided for my occupation, I used to write *Volunteer*; then, later, perhaps as a childish form of self-assertion, I put down the truth: *Meeting Coenraad*. It is extremely difficult to leave empty the space provided for the admission of a dreary existence. The pen hangs in mid-air. Actually, it doesn't matter what I write on that card. The clerk is interested only in numbers — on my passport and on my credit card. At the bottom, my signature *Lola Montez* is supposed to attest to the truth of the statements above it. A bellhop is summoned with the palm of a hand against a bell, he is given my room key, he picks up my one bag. I do not follow him. I wait. I stand stock still, expectant. In that break of (the clerk's) routine, a connection is made. It is then, after a moment's hesitation and another glance at my registration card, that he turns to the pigeon-holed wall behind him and locates, to his right, a sealed manila envelope with my (false) name on it, which he hands over to me wordlessly. Once in my room, with all the locks and bolts in place, I tear open the envelope, extract an issue of the *National Geographic*, in whose pages I find the (coded) message from Coenraad. Inside is also a smaller envelope containing money in the currency of the country.

This is the point I am driven towards — that exquisite instant when I receive word of our next meeting. I pack and unpack; find my way to airports, bus stations and railway terminals; shiver or swelter; go hungry or vomit in public toilets. Sometimes I travel half around the earth to decipher a message that instructs me to leave the next day for yet another distant destination.

That night at the King Edward Hotel, between me and my envelope, stood a long line of people, a convention of some kind. Men in turtle-necks and pipes; women in slacks and shoulder bags, all wearing plastic-covered name tags over the left breast. Those not in line milled about, the women coming up close to the men's chests to read their names, but men keeping their faces at a distance from female breasts, lowering their heads a little if necessary in order to read. A harassed clerk called for reinforcements, and from an office behind him, briefly glimpsed when the door opened, a young woman came to stand beside him. The line straggled. They were in no hurry to get into their rooms, these chatty men and women, mildly titillated by their (temporary) release from, I imagined, academic dust. Later I found out that they were botanists. Gradually I moved up the line. When, finally, the envelope was handed to me, I felt it to be alarmingly thin. To hide my panic I adopted an air of world-weariness, appearing to be bored with everything in sight, following the bellhop with my coat draped loosely about my shoulders as if it were mink.

I stood inside the open door while he switched on all the lights, adjusted the (unadjustable) thermostat, pulled at the drawn drapes, turned on the television, pointed to the towels in the bathroom. With coins ready in my hand, I tipped him, bolted the door, turned off the canned laughter on the TV. My hands trembled as I tore open the envelope. The contents seemed to stick to the sides.

With thumb and forefinger I extracted a four-page sheet, which I found to be a report on Dutch elm disease, reprinted from *The Canadian Journal of Botany* (Volume 6, number 4). On the front was a photograph of a lone, leafless tree, its branches stark against a barren landscape. Beneath the picture was the word *Victim!* The text was surprisingly emotional in its language, with allusions to death, dying, fatal fungus, deadly disease, wasting away, terminal state, *in extremis*, moribund, hopeless. In this welter of decay there was mention of a Saviour of the Elm not yet in sight. There was one note of hope: ... *new strain known as Quebec Elm ... that resists the blight....*

What was I to make of all this? Perhaps Coenraad was asking that I be alert to the problems of our situation and make proper interpretations. He admires my intelligence in this respect. For instance, in a *Geographic* article on the nomadic freedom of the Berbers of the Sahara, there was a picture of a little girl, aged about ten, absorbed in the quaint occupation of rocking a skin pouch full of goat's milk into butter. I noticed she was blind, although the text made no reference to her plight. Interpretation led me to a clinic for blind children in Tangier where Coenraad was acting as a salesman for a pharmaceutical company. The question still remained: where, in the problem of dead elms, was his message for me? I counted words on a line, lines on a page; the number of Latin terms. Nothing was revealed. Fatigue diverted a rising dread. Perhaps my mind would be clearer in the morning.

Going alone to sleep I have been in the habit of reading the literature of our trysts. For one thing, using the *National Geographic* for a code ensured that I always had something to read the first night in a strange bed. For another, I was able to familiarize myself with the *ambience* of our rendezvous, so that if we were forced to stay under cover, as the expression has it, I would have stories of the region for his entertainment. In Bangkok, I told Coenraad that every plot of ground has a spirit. When you build a house, you mustn't drive the spirit away or you'll meet misfortune. So you give the spirit a house to live in, out of doors, in the east corner.

We differed at the deepest level once on the interpretation of the marriage custom in Botswana. Bared to the waist as a sign of humility, the princess dances for the bridegroom. An ox's gall bladder is pinned to her hair to signify luck, and she grasps two slender spears and a knife, indications that she is prepared to enter another's clan. As the setting sun colors the Mdzimba Range, the bride's father, King Sabhusa, silently watches the slow-moving dance, which is accompanied by a haunting dirge. My lover said that humility in a woman was a good start for marriage; whereas I felt that the reference to a haunting dirge showed apprehension for the future. The day before a Chasidic wedding, I told him, women were hired to spend the day crying.

After that I put to memory only stories of an impersonal nature. If he had met me in Tikal I would have repeated a story told by the priest of the village of Xcobenhaltun, who also practiced black magic. *I was called by the gods before I was born. While my mother was carrying me, my father did an evil thing to her, and from the womb I struck him dead.* And always, while reading the magazine alone in a hotel room, I could see Coenraad's blunt fingers turning the very same pages, his eyes following the identical lines. I had visions of a pen poised as he deliberated over the passage with the message, then inserting the magazine into the manila envelope for me to pick up at our next rendezvous. The botany reprint in my hands tonight fell to the floor. I had no wish to read again of the death of elms.

Now I was ready for the final part of my nightly ritual. Under a small ring of light on the night table was my pack of postcards, secured by a wide elastic band stretched to its limit, apparently, for it snapped as I removed it. First I shuffled the cards. Then I lay back against the pillows, closed my eyes and extracted at random three postcards.

The first card I drew was a photograph in sepia of a statue of a horse and rider. This was the only card I had to remind me of the Paralelo Hotel in Barcelona. There had been a knock on the door in the middle of that night, whispers in the hall, and a gentle coercion that I hurry and dress, we must leave immediately. In our hasty exit, in the lobby I managed to snatch a postcard off a rack on the counter. Two prostitutes in Fellini tight skirts and blouses, with thighs and breasts revealed, coming in at that hour with their customers, stared in disbelief at my theft, and continued to stare, unsmiling, while the two men joked and laughed, until the elevator doors closed on their disapproving faces.

Details of our short-lived passion in Barcelona are easily recalled but they give me small pleasure. Perhaps it was due to my discomfort in that seedy hotel. Water dripped down the walls; the bed clothes were damp. The war in Vietnam had not been going too well. I guessed that tighter security had been ordered, since we had begun to meet in working-class districts. In that airless, cramped room, with a cracked bidet opposite a sagging bed, I experienced a foreboding, a feeling as in childhood of something being wrong, or of some wrongdoing I was not aware of and of imminent punishment, in the course of which I would be apprised of my crime.

– I want to bear your child, I announced.

– Good God whatever for!

– So that no matter what happens, I will have our child to remind me always of our love.

– In Hiroshima you said it was an awesome act to bear children, terrible responsibility, things like that.

– I had forgotten.

The room was stifling. The lower half of the only window was blocked by an air-conditioner that didn't work; the upper half couldn't be pried open. The door, of course, was locked. And then Coenraad made me swear by the lives of the children I already have, that I was not, nor would I permit myself to become, pregnant. By him.

– Now, don't get upset, he added. Then standing back for a long look at me, he made a short speech about how women trapped men by having children. I think he used the words *foist upon*.

All the same, Coenraad subsequently wore a condom, especially designed, he said, to heighten my pleasure. The exact description on the box was 148 raised pleasure dots and eleven rings. Sometimes I wondered if its true purpose was prophylaxis against betrayal.

The rest of that short night was spent in the enjoyment of music. Coenraad rang downstairs and soon a young man appeared with a guitar. He strummed a melody as if asking Coenraad to savour the bouquet of the instrument. He continued to display his virtuosity for quite some time, then handed his instrument to Coenraad with a final surge of chords and a low bow. Oddly enough, the guitar was no prop, as the cornet was on a sultry night in New Orleans. Coenraad played beautifully, with rubato rhythms, controlling the melody with a seductive emphasis at the end of each phrase. Then he played *Recuerdos de la Alhambra* by Tarrega, entirely from memory, all the while holding my eyes with his, until I was brought to tears with the beauty of it all.

At two in the morning, as if he anticipated that tap on the door, Coenraad told me,

– It's understood that if there is no envelope from me, it means I cannot meet you.

– You mean, something will have happened to you!

– Not necessarily. Whatever the reason, it will simply mean I cannot see you.

– Cannot, or will not?

– It is the same.

The rider pictured on the stolen postcard was demanding my attention. On the reverse side, in three languages, it said he was a Catalonian king, *Ramon Berenguera*. He sat astride his mount, erect and imperious, cloak thrown back, holding the reins with one gloved hand, the other upraised in command. The sculptor had carved onto his face an expression of superiority over all he surveyed. That noble mien, I knew, could twist suddenly into rage. He reminded me of Zbigniew, my husband.

Quickly, I drew another card.

As I contemplated the second postcard, I wondered if I ought to continue in this manner of gambling on a night's sleep, since each card pointed to desolation. In looking at the picture of the house where Christopher Columbus spent his childhood, I recalled my feelings about Genoa. In the shabby alleys I had passed sombre men and women. Even the children on their way to school walked with a slow, serious gait. And in my hotel, the chambermaid, clothed in black from neck to toe, kept her face averted from me, her head bent over an armful of linen. Still, I knew she was onto me. I suspected she had examined the contents of my suitcase. My extra black dress would not have impressed her: she who had to wear black. Poor, overworked, supporting Lord knows how many, returning home at night to unmade beds. I offered her a pair of nylons. She took them out of my hand without a word, her face indifferent. I cannot bear indifference from anyone.

I pandered with perfume; she saw through me: I was lonely. Moreover, she sensed that I didn't have enough money or class or whatever it takes to be her superior. In Italian, I asked her name and told her mine. She continued making up the bed, replacing smooth clean sheets with smooth clean sheets, never raising her head. I felt I was in her way, even though I sat in a corner on a chair with my feet up. In the bathroom, the sample bar of soap, already dwindled to a sliver, was left to lie in its puddle. I told myself, you haven't guts enough to buy yourself a regular-size bar of scented soap to show your independence. Tonight you will struggle with what's left of the hotel soap, lathering with it as best you can, using your hands to wash yourself, since the towels were removed and not replaced. You have been left with one small piece of linen for the bidet. You deserve no more, since your lack of authority encourages the poor girl to steal your share of the allotted soap. Why do you not assert yourself, demand what is coming to you, so we would both have more respect for ourselves? Instead, I pretended to read.

The morning after Coenraad's visit the same maid lingered in our room. She smiled and looked up every once in a while as she changed the wrinkled stained sheets. Rapid outbursts of information. I did not answer her, because I was at the window, unseeing, deaf to everything but the echo of last night's endearments. I was led by her to a chair and eased into it with the gentlest of touch. When she left, she walked backwards, her arms cradling the sheets. In the bathroom were two wrapped bars of soap, two washcloths and four large towels. Too late. I wanted to hang on to all the juices and all the odors. I wanted never to wash again.

The last postcard for the night was one of Aberdeen Harbor in Hong Kong, showing its waters as a mass of junks and sampans and two restaurants, painted vermillion, all ostensibly floating. I recalled I just had time for a five-minute ride on a sampan, ferried by a small, thin woman of indefinite age who concentrated on the watery space she opened up for herself and whose small children huddled in one corner so that I was drawn again and again to stare back at the three pairs of accusing eyes. Although it was a brief experience, I feel I know a great deal about people whose entire lives are spent on a tiny open boat. In fact the young man in charge of the eleventh floor of our hotel was born and raised on a junk. He had many stories to tell me in the idle afternoons when we sipped tea at his station opposite the elevators.

It was at the Hong Kong Hilton that I made another attempt to gain a more secure place in Coenraad's life. One night we were arm in arm at the picture window, high above the harbor, watching the red and green and white lights of the ferry boats and steamers and the American Seventh Fleet. I was thinking particularly of Sundays at home when Zbigniew comes back from the stables, hangs up his riding crop beside the mantel-piece and settles in with the week's newspapers. The memory of what follows, every Sunday of the year, year after year, made me shudder. I announced to my lover then and there, at the window, that I was willing to move to Boston. Perhaps, some day . . . he and I could . . .? He turned and looked at me through slitted eyes, the palms of his hands together at his chest. He bowed.

– It is written that one meeting is worth ten partings. Yet one parting is of greater consequence than ten meetings. For if lovers keep regular hours, then meetings and partings are as the comings and goings to the supermarket.

Fortunately, I can take evasiveness for an answer. Otherwise we would engage in a tennis match of accusations and denials, denials and accusations, back and forth, interminably. Just the same I wished he would consider my point of view. A straight *yes* or a *no*. I'm tired of having to interpret. Some instinct, though, cautions me to avoid ultimata. My defeats are numerous enough without inviting more. Possibly I said,

– I live in a nice house, you know. My house is in a nice part of Toronto. I hate disorder. Every time I leave I clean and straighten the drawers. The laundry is done; the plants are watered. Every time I go away I leave the house in good shape. I miss putting things in order.

Perhaps he replied,

– My work is hazardous, but there's a good pension after twenty years with The Agency. I think I'll take up golf when I retire. The children will be gone by then, I'll probably be lonely, but there will be grandchildren. I am looking forward to that. Elfrida is getting married in June, did I tell you, a week after her graduation?

Suddenly a door slams and I am eleven years old. It is February and I stand in a cold rain. The landlady is in the doorway and says, You don't live here any more; go find your mother. And slams the door shut.

In our eagerness, Coenraad and I had undressed so quickly our clothes were all over the room. I began to tidy up. I placed pairs of shoes under the bed, I hung up his English costume of gray flannels and blue blazer. I put his bowler hat on top of the dresser. I folded, hung and straightened until order was restored. Only then was I able to return to the pleasures of that hotel room.

Yet, despite Coenraad's passionate embraces, despite kisses and endearments, despite everything, my mind dwelt only on the furnishings of the room. I stared at the walnut veneer of the dressers, the dot of light in the television glass, the Swedish sphere overhead and the five chrome lamps of different sizes strategically placed about the room. On the wall opposite, appearing and disappearing with the motion of Coenraad's body above me, were three watercolors painted on rice paper, of lotus blossoms in the rain, two small birds on a snowy branch and a bamboo grove. The *décor* was an intriguing theme of East meeting West, or, as Auden defined poetry, the juxtaposition of irreconcilable elements. I was about to expatiate on the phenomenon of paradox, when I remembered that my philosophizing causes Coenraad to lose his erection. I lay still. Soon I was free to turn on my left side. Silent stars were visible through the window.

I must have fallen asleep with the postcard in my hand, for a sharp edge against my face woke me during the night. In the morning, I knew that my dreams had been satisfying, although I could not remember them. I woke with vague, contented thoughts. That I was. That Coenraad was. That it was all necessary. Such certainty evaporated when I was about to leave the room. Before venturing out, I spilled the contents of my purse on the dresser top. Item by item I picked up and replaced into zippered safety: my passport (false) which says my name is Lola Montez and that I was born in New York, New York, in the United States of America, on May 11, 1925, and shows a picture of me taken three years ago, which is still a reasonable likeness; my international credit card, good for another eight months; my travellers' cheques in various American-dollar denominations. Into the easily accessible centre pocket went a comb, hand mirror and lipstick, toothbrush, a packet of tissues, chewing gum and an extra pair of hose, as well as the hotel's *Key to Toronto* to be examined over breakfast. In the outer compartment I placed the botany reprint. In this section also there was a pen and a writing tablet, on the first page of which was the opening of a letter. *My dear darling children . . .*

I would continue the letter when I had decided what to write. Something had to be said. They were entitled to a communication from their mother. And if I worded it precisely, the letter might spare them a guilt they would always feel even though the fault is mine. Hidden deep inside this outer pocket was a smaller zippered one in which I kept their pictures, taken when they were small and when I was full of determination.

In this secret place also was a newspaper clipping, the print faded along its creases, torn from last spring's Paris edition of the New York *Herald Tribune*. It showed Coenraad being decorated by President de Gaulle. The President was a head taller than my lover, yet, in that stalwart glance of his, as he looked up past de Gaulle's right shoulder, Coenraad gave the impression he was the same height as the man who was pinning a medal on him. I presumed that the two young lads and a young girl, taller than everyone except the President, were Coenraad's children; and that the patrician woman at their side was his wife. She, Coenraad's wife, whose features have been bred small, her hair thick and her ankles slim. If he knew I had this picture, Coenraad would demand that I destroy it, since there must be no evidence to connect him with me.

Before leaving, I looked about the room to remember what I must return to. The small room was well laid out and contained, without crowding, a double bed, two chairs, two bedside tables, a large dresser and three lamps. The television set occupied an entire corner and was placed directly opposite the doorway, so that it was the first thing one saw on entering. It could be viewed comfortably while lying in bed. I considered living in a hotel room like this, where I could come and go unnoticed, but the faded mustard and olive green drapes and matching bedspread and shag rug would all have to be changed. On the other hand, the moment one thinks of improvements, other dissatisfactions crop up, and then one does not want to live there any more. The long, old-fashioned window, held together, it seemed, by a mesh of tiny wire hexagons, looked out on two skyscrapers, the CN Tower and a patch of lake.

At this time of the morning in all hotels the automatic lift stops at each floor to pick up men in gray suits, white shirts and blue or maroon ties, who smell of lotions and pomades, who keep a tight grasp on their attache cases, who crowd against one another and against me.

– That sexy singer is on again tonight, wanna go?

– Naw. She's full of shtick.

– Everybody's gotta have a shtick.

– Yeah, well, I've seen hers.

Then, a moment before they touch down in the lobby, a change comes over their faces, which, from the start, had displayed a certain irascibility — seconds before the elevator stops, their heads tilt forward, there is a shuffling of feet. Here, now, at the King Edward, at eight o'clock in the morning, I was alone in the elevator all the way from the fourteenth to the main floor. The lobby was empty except for a man in a brown suit in a big leather chair, looking down his cigar, bringing it to his mouth slowly and regularly. Coenraad never smokes, not even for professional reasons.

It was a relief to get out into the streets crowded at this hour with people going to work, or leaving for home after a night shift. It was a relief, almost, to be assailed by fumes of monstrous trucks. I stopped at the kiosk on the sidewalk in front of the O'Keefe Centre, read announcements of plays and concerts, and stared at photographs of actors and musicians unknown to me. I go only to movies, where I can slip into the dark at any time. Outside the Union Station images came to me of my war-time voyeurism at sixteen, when I went on Saturdays and Sundays and holidays to watch the tearful partings and reunions. I remembered especially the children. They hovered near a parent, their eyes bright with fear. They pretended pride of luggage, saying they would watch it, served by an intuition that where there are possessions there is home; that they would not be left behind so long as they stayed close to the suitcases. Tears sprang to my eyes as I considered my present loneliness, similar to that of my youth; now, as then, they were tears of longing for an absent lover.

At that precise instant it came to me what Coenraad's message was: the street was Elm and the number of pages of the botany bulletin, four, pointed to the street number as possibly four or forty or four hundred. All at once, pangs of hunger replaced my anxiety. Across the street was the Royal York Hotel, which looked as formidable as it did in the days when I stood in awe of large buildings. Because of the heavy traffic, I crossed the wide boulevard with difficulty; at one point I stood on an imaginary island of safety while cars and taxis drove on either side of me.

Steps retraced, it soon became apparent, led to fears recalled. I felt I was going to be asked to leave this huge, hushed lobby with its many lamps and dark wood, its deep red carpeting buried under soft sofas and chairs. Then my attention was caught by a board at one end of the long reception desk. There were numbers in sequence on the board, room numbers probably, and over some of the numbers a little light was blinking rapidly. The same numbers over the key slots were also lit up. Thus, at a glance, one knew immediately whether there was a message or mail. For the first time I preferred the mechanical to the personal. The humiliation of having to approach, obsequiously, an indifferent clerk, to ask, over a period of many clays, and several times a day, for word from Coenraad — that form of debasement would be obviated.

Here, as elsewhere, unless I clearly revealed what was regarded as wealth, position, or, at the very least, respectability, I came under scrutiny, direct and indirect, from everyone. This was no time to prevail. I enquired, Where is the coffee shop? And here, as elsewhere, there was obvious relief in the reply, You must go downstairs, follow the signs. The basement rotundas were bright with overhead fluorescent lights and a practical carpet of orange and red circles set in squares of blatant blue. This confirmed my theory that all carpets in hotels all over the world were either orange or red or a combination of the two colors, and all in geometric patterns. The wallpaper in the coffee shop was a duplicate of the floor. Inside the entrance was a sign on a floor stand, Please Wait To Be Seated.

I followed the hostess who was dressed, like myself, in a basic black dress with pearls. She held a clutch of menus to her breast. I followed her as she made her way between small square tables towards the wall opposite and turned left. I saw I was being led to the end table next to the supply station where waitresses were milling about, clattering spoons and filling glasses with water. For a long time I have suspected that when I come alone into a restaurant I am going to be seated next to swinging kitchen doors or behind bins for dirty dishes. In contrast, when Coenraad and I enter a dining room there is a snapping of fingers and a scurry to seat us at an advantage. The hostess halted before a table laden with dirty plates; a cigarette stub was in the ketchup. I decided to stop following on her heels and fell back. She must have sensed what was, for me, a kind of rebellion, for she suddenly wheeled about and led me to a seat at a window at the other end. She put one of her cards on the table before returning to her place behind the sign.

In front of me appeared a glass of water; to my right the cup was lifted and filled with hot coffee, even as I was reading the menu. I was aware of someone in a white apron over a blue dress, standing at my chair, probably the waitress, her pencil poised over a pad, but I hesitated to give my order. Truth was, I felt I should not be here. There is something indecent in eating breakfast in public. It's like getting out of bed in a roomful of strangers. Keeping my eyes on the printed cardboard, I ordered Breakfast Number Four, consisting of juice, porridge, bacon and eggs, toast, jam and coffee. Whatever lies ahead, my mother used to say, a good breakfast will see you through. Every morning with her eyes on the clock she would become impatient with my lack of attention; alternately she urged me to eat more and to stop eating because she would be late for work. As I looked up to give my order, I thought the waitress must have risen very early, while it was still dark, to be ready, all combed and starched and white shoes cleaned, to serve me at this hour. Perhaps she has a child to take to the day nursery on her way to work. I can see them, mother and child, still somnolent, she pulling the little girl, who has difficulty keeping up with her mother. They take buses and subway, she, the child, being pulled on and off. There will be a return trip, reversing the direction. In winter it will again be dark as they make their way home, the mother tired and walking not so quickly, the child chattering, the mother not listening, so that whatever is significant at that moment to the four-year-old girl will disappear from her memory forever, perhaps to be recalled in dreams that will seem to be without meaning.

When the table was cleared, except for the coffee cup, which I asked to be refilled, I spread out the map. Streets were listed on the back. I suffered a seepage of self-confidence. Which of the streets named Elm was I supposed to locate? There were not only two Elm Streets, but Elm everything else — glen and grove, crest and place, square, bank, avenue, dale, manor, lane and road. I counted twenty-six in all. I brought out the botany reprint, hoping to find a phrase or a sentence that would reveal a more precise location. The only place named was Quebec. *The new strain, known as Quebec Elm, from its origins at L'Assomption, north of Montreal, resists the blight that will eventually wipe out the American elm.* I considered that Coenraad might have been in error, directing me to Toronto when he meant Montreal. Yet to doubt his knowledge of Canadian geography would be to doubt the man himself: he is his work, and his work is, in a sense, global. Any notion that I have a superior ability to read, interpret and deduce disappeared in the face of the hopelessness expressed in this scientific paper. Then it came to me that love has nothing to do with science, and that my first hunch was correct. The map showed an Elm Street downtown, north of Queen, between Yonge and Bay, within walking distance.

Even as I gulped the last of the coffee and crumpled the map I wondered how I would be able to wait for Coenraad in Toronto. The city is mined, for me, with the explosive devices of memory. In other places I await my lover with a degree of equanimity because I know what I have to look forward to. I can wait anywhere. I have learned to sit still, to stand still, to remain silent. I eat and sleep and I wander the streets. To help put in the time while waiting I take long walks. Wherever I am, I set out thinking the air will do me good, which is untrue in London or Mexico City or Los Angeles, but the habit is strong and I march along believing the excursion will prove salubrious. I don't use maps; I don't worry about getting lost. I make turns recklessly: a right turn here, a left there. Walking in circles has become a skill. This is to avoid the monotony of merely stepping on and off curbs.

Venice provided me with endless turns, many leading to little curved bridges, where I would stop exactly midway and take in the view from both sides. Invariably I leave the main thoroughfare and find myself, in the cities of Europe, on narrow cobbled streets. In America it is more difficult to create diversions while walking, since the streets are laid out in simple blocks that often lead only to a gas station or a shopping mall. Sundays, however, I take no walks; Sundays fill me with despair. I hang about the hotel, in my room or in the lobby, until the museums open. Sunday is a family day. It is on Sunday that husband and wife and children go out for a walk, the youngest daughter at her father's side. And in Paris, I observed, husband and wife take a promenade when they are old, his arm linked in hers, resting in a cafe, where they order rich cakes.

In other cities I walk endless hours in palaces and art galleries and libraries and museums. I feel at home in public buildings. Their doors, by law, must be open on specified days, at specified hours. Their doors, old or new, are on well-oiled hinges and await only a slight shove or a light pull to open. Once inside, I am free of all responsibilities: it is requested only that I do not smoke or spit on the floor. I surrender to the seduction of stale air and the subtle persuasions of the dead. I am invited to love the Gutenberg Bible or the *Guernica* or a wooden Japanese saint, circa 1132. I become an arbiter of taste, a patron. And when my eyes can no longer focus and my mind no longer has preferences, I am at liberty to leave.

Coenraad cannot comprehend the art of waiting. Often, when we were sitting up in bed, shoulders and legs touching, he asked me,

– When did you get here?

– Three days ago.

– And what have you been doing?

– Waiting.

– Yes, but what did you do?

– I told you, I waited.

– You must have done something — you ate, you slept, you took a shower. What else?

– I walked to the Louvre. I took the train to Versailles.

– He is not aware of the activity involved in waiting for him.

It takes a great deal of energy to wait. Although I am quiet, I feel as if I were running all the while to a point in the distance, panting for breath. My entire being strains towards that moment when he will appear. Time is suspended; it goes on without me. And then, at the sight of him, in one split second, the waiting comes to an end: the clocks start their wild clacking, their hands race towards the time when he will go back out the door. And then, the instant the door closes behind him, the instant I am alone again, when I see the empty pillow beside me, there begins that exquisite longing to be with him again. The yearning starts and ends my days. As for Coenraad, he said that once, when he was in danger, he told himself, if I get out of this alive, I will never let her go. But of course he did. Over and over. Still, I have become accustomed to waiting. It's not so bad: I always have something to look forward to.

Despite the dreary morning, under a sky the color of ashes, people hurrying to work displayed a verve and buoyancy I found stimulating. The men were freshly shaven, the women's lipstick was unblemished, all had clean shirts and fresh blouses. A momentum carried them towards one building or another, into which they disappeared with an eagerness I knew they couldn't maintain past the first coffee break. Tenacity of purpose remains with their middle-aged employers, who precede them by one hour in the morning and depart one hour after they have left. These reflections came to mind as I began to pass familiar buildings. I was walking north on Bay Street, on the east side, keeping to my right. On the other side of the street many changes had taken place. Another skyscraper was going up. Gone was the Canadian Pacific Railway and Steamship office at the corner of King Street, where, just before the war, I went with my mother to buy a ticket to sail on a Cunard liner to Marseilles. I went alone to see a father whom I didn't remember. But the Stock Exchange was still in the same place. I smiled again at the sight of its frieze of sturdy, stalwart laborers drilling, digging, pounding. Now there was a fried-chicken restaurant next door.

A few more steps brought me to 335 Bay Street, to Herbert House, where, years ago, I too went in at this time of the morning.

Here, on the ninth floor, I typed addresses all day long, every day and Saturdays to one o'clock. The sight of the recessed Art Deco entrance brought back the mood of those times, a vague unhappiness, not unlike the melancholy that now overtakes me when I am alone at night. I stopped to look down at the basement window of the coffee shop where I first met Max, but it was a barbershop now. From my desk in Herbert House I could see the sign across the street, *Savarin*, the letters spelled out vertically on the long sign. I spent many hours gazing at the large, rounded windows of the Savarin after Max took me dinner-dancing there one night. Beneath a dome painted midnight blue we held each other all night, pretending to dance. Under the same painted ceiling, with its plaster rosettes, vine leaves and wreaths, at one of those same curved windows, a month later at noon, I was the guest of Max's mother. The waiter led me across the dance floor, crowded during the day with tables and chairs. He led me along a wrought-iron balustrade, up two steps, to a small table where Max's mother was waiting. She greeted us with a smile, and thanked the waiter, whose first name she knew. She sat with her back to the window; her thick auburn hair, in a coil about her head, appeared as a halo. The full light of high noon was upon me. I looked across at Herbert House, counting the floors to the ninth (did the lobby count as the first?) and tried to guess which was my office window, the fourth or fifth from the end? I recall that I attempted to cut a soft white roll in half with a knife. Permit me, Max's mother said, and tore the bun delicately with her fingers and handed it back to me. The butter was hard and I implanted blobs of it into the soft dough. The chair was deep and in order to reach my food I had to sit forward on its edge. I ate the two rolls at once, by themselves, to the last crumb, to show my gratitude for her kindness.

Max's mother spoke to me of the war, of social problems, of friendship and of youth. My voice when I was young projected even less than it does now and my considered comments were lost in the noise. She toyed with her food — it was curried shrimp — but drank three cups of black coffee. I came to the bottom of my plate, a delicate white china with rose-colored flowers along the border. When I studied her features, I found her deep, brooding eyes to be exactly like her son's. My firstborn, she said of Max, with a smile exactly like his, even to the large front teeth and the rest of the teeth much smaller, not matching in color. At that sublime moment, when I recognized her to be the (beloved) progenitor of my (beloved) Max — at that exact moment, when I would have fallen at her feet and called her Mother, she began to speak of Maximilian, and her words had the remarkable effect on me of that heavy door being slammed shut again. I cannot quote her exactly, because my hold on events becomes shaky every time that door bangs, but I think the gist of it was something like this: Maximilian has a great future and I will not permit anything or anyone to stand in his way, especially the likes of you, he's simply a fool to have gotten himself involved, he thinks he's in love, he's at that age, I have nothing against you personally, I don't even know you, what's more I don't intend to, you're all wrong for him, wrong background, your mother works in a factory, there are men who are not your father living with her, use your handkerchief or tissue or whatever you can find in that cheap purse, you'll get over it, just in case you're scheming to see him anyway, I can tell you right now, I'm prepared to do anything to prevent that, even if I have to send him to his uncle in New York.

I never saw Max again. Not even after he was sent back by his uncle in a wheelchair, having broken his back in a dive onto a submerged rock, was I permitted to see him.

By this time Bay Street was busy with the final wave of office workers. It felt good to be carried along by the crowd. I set my face to imitate the faces around me, whose expressions I can only describe as a mixture of anxiety and indifference. We crossed as a pack at the lights at Adelaide Street and again at Richmond Street. Cars were unable to make any turns against our solid mass. A gust of wind at the corner of Queen Street forced me to take shelter in a hollow of gray stone. In this exact spot once stood a pawnshop whose door never opened and through whose blackened window nothing was visible. Everyone knew that the two old bachelor brothers, whom no one had ever actually seen, refused offers of millions for their miserable corner store. The brothers were probably carried out. (When we were forced to leave a condemned house, having lost the battle with cockroaches and rats, my mother cried, I don't want to leave my little palace.) In the refuge of the Simpson Tower I was joined by a swaying figure of a man, gray-stubbled, his eyes half-closed, muttering to himself. He was a ghost of the Depression mendicant who went with someone's dime to Child's for a bowl of hot soup. Suddenly I realized that in my obsession with vanished landmarks I had forgotten why I was walking these old streets. I had neglected to keep an eye — the third eye — open for Coenraad. I glanced at the man beside me. He was leaning into the curved stone and dozing. In order to give him every opportunity to make himself known, I edged slowly away from the Tower towards the crowd at the curb, watching him all the while. Coenraad's disguises are as varied and as inventive as those of artists at a Beaux Arts Ball. With the others I waited for a policewoman to blow a whistle and stop traffic in order to cross. When I got to the other side I looked back. He had disappeared. Possibly he was a wino who had gone into Simpson's to warm up.

Once inside Eaton's, I headed straight for the glove-and-scarf section. I could have found my way to any department blindfolded.

In the past, going to Eaton's was a day's holiday. We basked under bright lights and examined things we would buy if we had money. It was different now: I could choose any scarf I fancied. Yet, in spite of the elaborate displays, I saw nothing I wanted. Under the neon lights the synthetic bits of cloth looked cheap and shabby. A frail, elderly woman behind the counter asked if she could help, but I noticed that she was indifferent to my reply. I sensed she was acting out a paid role for a hidden camera.

– I want a pure silk scarf, blue, the same blue as in this tweed, I told her, at the same time extending the lapel of my coat towards her.

– Everything we have is out on the counter.

– Look in the drawers, I used to be able to buy special things that were hidden in drawers.

– Everything we have is out on the counter.

Such inane repetition, I thought, meant that the monitor was equipped for sound. I saw also that beyond giving a token performance, she would do no more. I turned to leave when a voice in my ear said,

– Where are the silks of yesteryear . . . ?

A derelict in prop clothes, in a stained green jacket, too long in the sleeves, loose trousers held up somehow, was standing beside me, and as he breathed in my face, which I turned towards him, he repeated, Ah, those silks of long ago. . . . He drew himself up and buttoned the one button on his jacket. It came to me that he was not drunk, his breath was sweet. He stood beside me with an air one might call aristocratic. It was all too wonderful: Coenraad as a downtown wino! Certain that I was being observed by the hidden camera, I took care not to react with the joy that was overwhelming me, lest I blow his cover. I made the obligatory gestures: I pretended to recoil, I tightened my lips in outrage. He took my hand from the counter up to his lips. At the same time as he bent his dirty, matted brown hair over the back of my hand, he raised his bloodshot eyes to mine and winked. I was reminded again of the consummate artistry in the design of contact lenses. The saleswoman forgot the spy camera and came darting out from behind the counter to avert what she probably believed would become a disturbance. I waved her back to where she belonged.

– Think nothing of it, I told her. It is the custom in Vienna. Men do this from force of habit. Do not mistake gallantry for desire.

To the consternation of all the clerks, and perhaps the person who monitored the TV, as customers gasped and gaped, I put my arm through his and together we marched down the aisle to Queen Street.

We walked in silence. We rarely speak when we are in public — he because he must be on the *qui vive* at all times, and I because his presence renders me speechless. Elm Street was in the opposite direction, yet I did not question why we were heading west on Queen instead of north on Yonge. Explanations between us are unnecessary: even in sleep we understand one another. At Bay, I looked up at the old City Hall tower and noted it was ten o'clock. That quick glance, no longer in duration than the jab of a needle, released a flow of images. Of green corridors and brown battle-ship linoleum with that morning's footprints making a gray path down the middle; of hours on a hard oak bench outside a room closed off by a door of frosted glass, with a design in clear glass of a bouquet of flowers tied with two flowing ribbons. The sign on that door, Juvenile Court, was painted in straight black letters in two horizontal lines across the flowers. Perhaps it was coincidence, but at the same instant as my mother's weeping face passed before me he grasped my hand and gave it a reassuring squeeze. I caught Coenraad looking down at me and wondered if he noticed how long my hair had grown since that time in Montreal when he said he did not like it short.

Further on, near St. Patrick, the same plucked chickens, it seemed, still hung head down in the window of A. Stork and Son. The small red brick building, I noticed now for the first time, had a perfect symmetry. A stone inserted under the peak of the roof had a date on it: 1881. The haphazard growth of this old part of town was revealed in the many stores selling used furniture and used clothing and used comic books and even used pornography. Behind a dirty window, in front of a dirty gray cotton curtain, was a sign, *Madame Olga, Gypsy Fortune Teller*, printed on a fly-specked piece of cardboard. Beneath, in smaller letters, She will tell you Past, Present and Future. Are you looking for peace of mind? Are you unlucky in love, marriage or work? Then come see Madame Olga. She will remove all evil influence and bad luck. Coenraad halted. For a moment I thought we were going in to have our fortunes told. Even though his own life is dictated by the implacable Agency, Coenraad is convinced our love for one another was predestined. As for me, I was eager to have my future foretold. But it was the door next to Madame Olga's that we entered. I hesitated while he started up a long flight of steep stairs. His heels were worn right down. He walked bent over, head jutting forward from a rounded back. Once he stumbled. Perhaps he was just staying in character; my lover is sure-footed and always walks upright. He held open a steel fire door and waited for me. We entered a brightly lit factory. Rows of women's dark heads were bent over whirring sewing machines. On either side of where we stood were long tables laden with bolts of brilliantly colored silks.

At our entrance, a young woman nearest the door stopped her machine, nodded her head in a gesture of recognition, then went along a narrow aisle between the worktables towards the back, where she opened a plywood door set into a plywood partition. She came out immediately, followed by a tall man who, in contrast to her robust youth was vague in his grayness: his hair, face, the suit he wore, all created so ethereal an effect I was surprised to hear a voice. He addressed Coenraad in a language I didn't understand. I remained perfectly still, trusting Coenraad, who sometimes has me play a small part in his work. Coenraad said, in English,

– Here she is. I'll be back later.

Then he who I thought was Coenraad brought his worn heels smartly together, raised my hand once more to his lips and said,

– Dear lady, it has been most agreeable. Here you will find what you are looking for.

It was apparent I had been taken in, after all, by the man's fine manners. Am I a child, always confusing hopes with facts? I wondered. The steel door was closing on its pneumatic rod behind me.

– Now then, said the owner or whoever he was, have a look at these materials, pointing to a long plywood table with silks, we can make up any style you like, squares, oblongs, triangles, large and small. Lowest prices in the city.

– Who was that man? I asked, still uncertain.

– Laszlo? He is my countryman. Any business he brings my way, he receives compensation. Now, how many dozen? what kind of business? boutique, department store, beauty parlor? extra discount for quantities above two dozen.

– There's been a mistake. I want only one scarf, a blue one, for this coat.

– Laszlo is never mistaken, he is my countryman. I know him very well. He is sensitive. He can recognize a buyer immediately. Comparison shopping, were you? You won't find more beautiful silks anywhere. These are from France, flown to Miquelon, they find their way to Montreal, if you comprehend my meaning, and then are sent to me by another countryman. That's why I can sell silk scarves at the prices I do.

The women at the machines looked up every once in a while with interest. They spoke quietly to one another, yet obviously made themselves heard above the noise for they often laughed. I wanted to stay in this room of rainbow silks shining in the light of a dozen neon tubes. I was tempted to beg to be put to work, to be given a social insurance number, to belong with these smiling women. I could learn their language, I could fit in, I felt, I had been one of them a generation ago, I know this district, I know exactly where to go for a paper cup of coffee that will spill over on top of the bagel with cheese in a bag. But all I managed to do standing there was to convey in dumb show the fact that I was not who he thought I was. At that he propelled me, almost pushed me, along the aisle back to his office. No sooner were we behind the door than he grasped my wrists in his two hands and forced me to my knees. Red spots appeared high on his waxen cheeks; light came into the flat yellow eyes. I stayed on my knees, waiting.

– Who are you, who sent you, how did you find me?

Just as suddenly, he released his hold on me. He fell back into a chair, his hands hung loose at his side, his face became pallid again.

– Thank God I have been caught at last.

I remained on my knees, helpless in the sight of his intolerable pain. Come, I told myself, stop for a moment. Your pursuit of love will wait half an hour. And by the time he discovers what a coward you are in the presence of pain, you will have gone. Comfort him if you can. And don't worry about consequences: you are a stranger to him no matter who he thinks you are; whatever it was that had happened, it had nothing to do with you and you cannot be blamed.

– Tell me, *Tatele*, who is after you, what crime did you commit?

– Ghosts. No one was left alive. I am the only one and I do not want to live. There is no one, no one to forgive me. I dream of an avenging angel who will confront me with my sin. Only death will end my nightmare.

It was my intention to raise my eyes to his in sympathy and understanding, but my gaze was arrested by an old crackled photograph being held before me. It was a picture of a small dark woman, who stared out with the knowledge of her fate in her eyes, the look that comes, as I have seen in similar pictures, when all fear is gone and only the certainty of death remains.

– Imagine, he said, how accurate the Germans were, that when the Red Cross found Miriam's final photograph in a cabinet in an office in Warsaw after the war, they knew at once whose wife she had been.

One hand was stroking my hair. He could not have known I was immobilized by the touch of his hand on my head. No one had ever done that. But then, I had never been on my knees before.

– In the middle of the night the Nazis came. I was half asleep, waiting for Miriam to come back to bed. She was attending to the children in the other room, they had bad colds and were feverish and she was up every four hours with the alarm clock to give them aspirins. I had no thoughts when I heard banging on the door and shouting in German. I mean to say, I have no recollection of deciding to abandon my family to their fate. All I can tell you, all I have been able to tell myself, is that my body had a will of its own. I jumped out the window of our bedroom. I ran. Once my body knew it was safe in the forests it knew so well, my mind, no, worse, my imagination, took over and has never ceased to this moment. Over and over I see my brave, frightened Miriam, my Yankel and little Shmuel being taken away, the children half asleep, their noses running from their colds. I see Miriam fingerprinted, tattooed, photographed, filed and gassed. Day and night I have prayed that God punish me, but He chose His own means to scourge my soul. I prospered. I don't care about money, yet it keeps accumulating. I give away as much as I can to orphans, to the lonely and the sick; I turn no one away. I have been publicly honored. At last God took pity on me. This body that betrayed me in youth is being punished in old age. These arrogant arms are feeble; these treacherous legs have lost their strength. One day I fell in a coma in the street. People thought I was drunk and stepped over me. The police came; I went willingly; I thought the uniformed men were Nazis come to reunite me with my wife and sons. I was not put in a camp; I was taken to a hospital; I was cared for as if I were deserving. I have diabetes, holes in my stomach that bleed; a heart that tightens with memories. With each new illness I bless God.

I lifted my face to his face; I took his hands in mine; he raised his eyes heavenward.

– You have been sent to be with me at the end. It is you who will forgive me.

Through my mind went a rush of responses. I was ready to point out that what he had done was natural and human, understandable and therefore forgivable; that he needed absolution from no one. I wanted to exhort him to forgive himself and forget, yet I knew that my arguments were useless: logic had nothing to do with his pain: the source of his anguish was beyond understanding: reason had nothing to do with his plight. Stay, stay, he was saying, I must hear words of forgiveness from someone. But he was not looking at me; his vision was elsewhere. In retrospect now, I think, that if he had not turned his back on me, if he had not turned to the wall, I might have stayed, for his sorrow made my agitations seem frivolous. But he had released me. He was facing the wall, wringing his hands, rocking in prayer, and from his throat, seemingly without breath, I heard Kaddish, the Aramaic ritual prayer for the dead, now clear, now lost in murmur, beginning with those terrible and necessary first two words, *Yisgadal V'yiskadash.* Simply, silently, briefly, I watched the figure in his communion with the dead. There was nothing for me to say. I had to leave.

Descending the dark, steep stairs I kept seeing the man's tragic face before me as an afterimage. If only I could write! I had the time; the many hours of waiting might well be spent in writing. I would buy a notebook and keep a pen in its spiral spine. When Coenraad and I are together, words are not necessary, yet the silence which can be so eloquent between us is unnerving when I am alone. Come to think of it, I have not been without imagination. I saved stories to entertain him with, and what didn't actually happen, I invented. He was astounded: Where do you meet such people? He worried that I was involved with them, not realizing that most of my characters were imagined, and the rest speculated upon. I always tried to be amusing. When he laughed or made love, Coenraad revealed himself to be a man of undisguised joy.

If I could write, where would I begin? Perhaps I could weave a story around some item in a newspaper. There, at the corner of Dundas, displayed behind a wire mesh in a padlocked box, was the *Toronto Daily Star*. In the left-hand column, which was edged with a black border, was a heading, *Murder or Suicide?*

– When Lewis B. Martindale came home Sunday night, he found his wife standing on a chair with a rope around her neck.

– I'm going to kill myself and you can't stop me, she said.

– Let me help you, he said, and kicked the chair from under her.

– I watched her die without regret, he said when questioned.

A writer would speculate on the circumstances that led to the wife's desperation and the husband's uninterest. No. I don't think I have the necessary objectivity to elaborate on such a piece of news.

Perhaps I ought to try my hand at fiction. I would have to be careful: for me the power of the written word is so great that there would be the danger of my believing what I imagined. And were it to be a love story, the hero would be Coenraad. Therein lay another problem: since Coenraad was always in disguise, in order to authenticate him, fictionally speaking, I would have to reveal him in his essential characteristics. I was not certain I wanted to do that. It was no use pretending that I could tell anyone else's story, so I might have to tell my own. For that I must rely entirely on memory.

In the midst of all this high resolve I realized that I am not permitted to put anything down on paper. That is the rule. There must be no papers, documents, letters, notes, journals or diaries that would expose our love affair.

At the very least, I should carry a pocket tape recorder for impressions and reflections. Or conversations overheard, as this one in the ward . . .

– How could you say such a thing!

– What . . . what did I say?

– You said, Every cell in your body has your name on it.

– It's true.

– Your tone of voice was insulting. You also said . . .

– Yes, yes, I know what I said. I tell you it does not matter what I say: that roses stink, that I will kill myself, that he is a man without pity. Words have nothing to do with him; he hears only a heavenly chorus singing his praises.

– He is so patient with you.

– Indifference is often mistaken for patience.

– He comes to see you every night.

– The weight of all that indifference!

– I thought I saw his right shoulder twitch.

– It doesn't twitch for me.

Nothing can be concealed from Coenraad: the tapes would be discovered. Nor would I be able to convince him that my tapes would be an innocent diversion, simply a means of putting in time. It was in a motel on a highway outside Hamilton, New York, that

I first broached the matter of having a small microphone to speak into when he is not with me. I had been alone for four days, unable to leave the motel. All around were overgrown fields closed off with barbed wire. There was only the highway and nothing to see but the neon motel sign and a few cars parked in front of doors. There was nothing to read except my copy of the *Geographic* with its article on the Finger Lakes. This did not fire my imagination. Coenraad said if I were to use a tape recorder he would never be able to trust me again. It was then he brought out his pocket tape recorder, found a tiny cassette under some shirts to insert into it. I heard a woman's gasps and the small screams that occur during that stage of lovemaking when her body claims its pleasures.

– Who, me?

– Listen . . .

– I don't remember . . . when?

– The first time. All the time.

– How do I know that's me.

– It's you. I don't sleep with anyone else.

When I stopped for a red light, a gambler's excitement seized me. If I were lucky, Coenraad would be waiting at Elm Place, only four blocks now along Spadina. Probability beckoned. I was reminded of the time I felt compelled to open a gate in a tiny garden in Kyoto. In that garden, three stepping stones and green moss on one side of the gate were the same as three stepping stones and green moss on the other. Still, I opened the gate and went through to the other side as if adventure awaited me.

Elm Place now was spelled out on a white metal plate on a post, in black letters in English and in Chinese. I reflected that my husband would be no more enamored of the resplendent Lucky Dragon on the corner than he had been of the Workmen's Labor League it replaced, the latter having been a pinochle-playing retreat for tired men whom Zbigniew accused of communist subversion, whereas I thought the only danger to society was in a slight redundancy in the name. Two blocks down, Elm Place crossed Kensington Avenue where once, when I was nine, I searched for the statue of Peter Pan. The old narrow houses still stood, separated only by painted drainpipes, but what had been parlors, inviolate, smelling of camphor and wax, never used except for weddings and funerals — these had been broken into and converted into stores. The tiny lawns were gone, their space taken up with crates of fruit and vegetables and barrels of pickles and herring. Guardians in heavy sweaters and thick boots stood out on the sidewalks. I saw their bare hands were blue with cold as they put money in the left pocket and made change out of the right pocket.

Number Forty was a bakery. Bread and rolls had been tossed onto an oilcloth-covered incline and had accumulated at the window's outer edges. As I opened the door, a bell was touched off: a superfluous summons: a woman was already waiting behind the counter. She was seated on a high stool, hunched over a newspaper spread out on the glass counter. One hand hovered over a large brass cash register; her other hand held a corner of the newspaper, ready to turn the page. She was taking her time acknowledging my presence. Finally she raised her head, gave me a quick glance and said, You're back, and continued reading. Perhaps she did know me, we were about the same age, although her face was more lined than mine and her hands work-worn. We might even have gone to Ryerson Public School at the same time.

I circled the small store, pretending to be making up my mind, all the while edging towards the rear, where I had seen a doorway screened off by a faded red velvet drape. Even though her eyes never left the newspaper, I sensed the woman was taking my measure. I wished I had on a printed rayon dress with a clean printed cotton apron over it, as she was wearing. I regretted being dressed in my black dress, the tailored tweed coat, the pearls. If you have grown up in these streets it is the act of a traitor to return smelling of expensive perfume and sporting the costume of another class. It isn't going away that causes resentment: after all, out of sight, out of mind. But once out of sight, I should stay out of sight. It is an unwritten law. Not only can you not *go* home again, you must not *come* home again. I took my time, going from kaiser rolls to onion buns, picking them out of wire baskets, pinching them as is the custom, keeping some and discarding others. One by one she brushed aside my selection with her forearm. Without looking up she knew when I had finished. She stopped reading, took a paper bag from under the counter, threw in the rolls, all the while shaking her head in what seemed to be disapproval. At what I had chosen? Still not looking at me she asked,

– What else?

Behind her was a wall of shelves laden with breads.

– What kind of bread have you got?

– White, black, *chalah*, Russian black, rye, double rye, with seeds, without seeds, water bread. What do you want?

– Give me a quarter of the Russian black.

Just as she turned to the shelf behind her, I detected a hint of triumph on her face. She had seen through me: I had tipped my hand: only those familiar with the enormous proportions of a Russian black bread know to ask for a segment. She cut through the thick crust, leaning heavily on the long knife. I pretended to drop all pretence.

– Listen, I said, I must find my husband. She would understand that. Maybe he rented a room here.

– Rent? What's to rent?

– Upstairs; or back of the store?

– Upstairs is an old widow, alone; in the back is my kitchen and my bedroom. She brought down a pan with brown cake. How about a nice piece honey cake?

– Is it fresh?

– Would I stand all day selling stale cake?

– All right, I'll take a slice. I want everything in plastic bags, separate.

– Plastic is a cent a piece.

She was forced to dump everything out on the newspaper. While she was preoccupied sorting, counting and adding, I made my way stealthily towards the curtained doorway at the rear. I had a glimpse of the interior, of a worn patterned linoleum and a dark wooden chair with the stuffing coming out of the leather seat.

– Get away from there or I am calling the police!

Her threat amused me. My mother used to call the police every Sunday, just after lunch, when the rest of the day stretched empty ahead. The police listened to her complaints, and to the counter-charges of the landlady, or another tenant, or from the man living with her at the time. They arrested no one. My mother heaped ancient curses upon their heads. Now the woman had left her counter and stood between me and the curtain in a stance of (familiar) outrage: legs apart, fist in the air, belly forward. At the same time she kicked a small gray cat that had ventured out beneath the drapes. What she and I both knew was that the next move was mine.

Then I saw it, the cash register, gilded to gleam like gold. There, at the end of the counter, beside the window, was the dowager of old brass cash registers, tall, ornate, square and round at the same time, with a keyboard of numbers and dollar and cent signs. I was drawn to it as a sleeper to a recurring dream. I rang up NO SALE. The drawer sprang open. She'd had a good morning. I plunged my hand into every compartment. First the pennies, then the nickels, dimes and quarters, and pitched them in all directions. Many of the coins landed at her feet. The impulse to vandalize the cash register was not born of the moment: the act had been waiting for me as an instrument waits for a performer. The cat scurried back under the curtain. I glanced at her to see what she thought of all this. Her manner had changed, I felt, to one of respect. Now the paper stuff: one-dollar bills, two fives and two tens, and one twenty-dollar bill, tossed in the air like confetti. I was exhilarated.

– *Nu*, are you satisfied, she asked quietly.

– Not quite.

– You've done enough, take your bread, go already.

– Tell me if there is any one waiting for me at the back.

– I told you . . . leave me alone.

– I want to see for myself.

She began to pick up the bills and straighten them one by one against the palm of her hand. She didn't say a word and her silence sounded like this:

What leads you to believe that I would permit you or any other customer who comes in for bread to go into the one place on earth where I can be a private person, how long do you think I would stay in business if I permitted such privileges? And my children, what kind of a mother would they say I am who cannot have a private life? And my husband, when he comes home from the factory and says what's new and I have to tell him there were lots of customers, but nobody bought anything, they just went into the back — how long do you think he would stay with a woman like that?

And in my disappointment, I might have replied:

What about me, do you think I've come all this way, six hours on the plane, just for bread? I'll eat the bread and then what? Nothing to show for all the trouble I've gone to!

All this time I remained perched behind the cash register while she was on her knees picking up coins. When she had a handful she rose and brought me the money, then went back and picked up some more. I was careful to put the coins and bills back in their proper compartments. I enjoyed being at the open cash register. Then, by tacit agreement, we resumed our rightful places on either side of the counter. She gave me a friendly smile.

– Stay, stay awhile, she said. She swept crumbs off the newspaper. Is today in the paper a true story like you wouldn't believe.

I saw that the masthead of the paper, the *Jewish Daily Forward*, had not changed.

– Tell me, I said, to show that I was no stranger to its contents, is Isaac Bashevis Singer still writing for *The Forward?*

– So you can read Yiddish!

– No, I read his books.

– Sit, sit awhile, she urged.

I sat where everyone sits in these bakeries — on the inside edge of the display window, first moving aside a straggling bagel. The height was comfortable; my feet were firmly on the floor. Moreover, if I stayed right here, at 40 Elm, perhaps Coenraad would find me. She read in a tone that suggested shock and wonder. Herewith the translation:

To the Editor and readers of *The Forward*:

I am a woman of seventy years, in good health, praise God, living in Buenos Aires, where I have been for the past fifty years. I have been blessed with children and grandchildren. My grandchildren beg to hear the stories, the same ones I used to tell their parents when they were young, about Poland where I grew up, about my beginnings in Argentina. Always I must be careful to stop the stories at my nineteenth birthday and go on from my twenty-first year. What happened in the time between is a dark secret I have revealed to no one, not even my late beloved husband, may he rest in peace. Throughout the years I have kept hidden what lies buried deep in my soul. Now, at the end of my life, I have a need to confess. As age takes its toll, I am afraid that one day I will blurt out the truth. That is why I write to you and to your many readers, so that the world will know what has weighed so heavily on my heart, and yet my children and their children will not suffer from that knowledge.

In my village in Poland, called Radom, there was an outstanding Talmudic scholar who, because of his great intelligence, was considered a most desirable match for some fortunate girl. It was understood that the eldest daughter of the richest man in town would become his bride. One day this brilliant, handsome student came to our little store to buy a schmalz herring. I was only seventeen. Even as I rolled up my sleeve to dip into the barrel, I caught him staring at my bare arm. To make the story shorter, we fell in love. A scandal! My dowry consisted of four pillowcases and, as the eldest daughter, I would someday inherit my mother's silver candlesticks. But Avrom didn't care, he was a modern man, who wanted to marry for love. We got married. Our future did not look good. My husband knew only what was written in the *Talmud*. How could he earn a living and help look after my widowed mother and my three little sisters?

At that time, just before the First World War, many young men were leaving for America. But you had to be healthy, and Avrom wasn't: he had spots on his lungs. So we went to Zurich instead, where the mountain air would be good for him. Not only that, but Switzerland was a haven for all who sought change of one kind or another — communists, anarchists and dadaists. For Avrom it was the perfect environment. He became a student at the University and I got a job in a watch factory. It was clean work but the hours were long. On Sundays, Avrom tried to teach me to read and write, but I was too tired to learn. Sometimes I went with him and his intellectual friends to concerts and plays. In the theatre one night, weary as I was, I became absorbed in a play called *A Doll's House*. That night I wasn't able to sleep. How could Nora leave that nice big house! How could she abandon her children to servants! For the rest of the night, Avrom tried to make me understand. She had to be free, he said. To go to work, like me? Just the same I listened attentively as Avrom explained the reasons Nora had to leave. She had to express herself as an individual. After that I began to observe the women of Zurich. They had cut their hair, they sat in cafes smoking cigarettes, they went out alone at night, they laughed a great deal. For me there was only hard work, misunderstandings and miscarriages. On my nineteenth birthday I, too, slammed a door. After the divorce, the Red Cross gave me money to go back to my family in Poland.

I had been given a first-class compartment on the train. I sat opposite a fine gentleman, with delicate hands and thick dark hair. Not so young, but not too old. He was very kind, bought me coffee and a box of chocolates. As the train sped past lakes sparkling in the sun, as we left behind the magnificent Swiss Alps, I had a vision of the harsh life awaiting me in Poland — a life of poverty and the dirt and disease that go with it. I burst into tears. He asked if there was something he could do for me. I told him exactly what you have just read. He understood: he too came from a kind of ghetto, the slums of Santa Rosa in Buenos Aires, where those of Indian descent lived. He described the many hardships and tragedies he had endured. Even though he was now a wealthy importer, he had never forgotten his early life. His wife had died young. He told me about his two motherless girls. It so happened, he told me, he was looking for a European governess for his children. He offered me the position. But I cannot read or write, I confessed. You are obviously very intelligent and will learn Spanish quickly, he replied. We had been conversing in French, a working knowledge of which I had literally acquired in my sleep from Avrom's comrades, who had often argued all night in the one room we lived in. We had arrived in Munich where Hector and I had to change trains. It took very little persuasion for me to take a train to Hamburg with him instead of going on alone to Warsaw.

In Hamburg we had to stay overnight as our boat was not due to sail for Argentina until the next day. I had my own room in an elegant hotel called *Vier Jareszeiten*, where the bathroom was as large as my home in Radom. In the afternoon we took a short pleasure cruise along the Elbe River in a ship called *Die Alte Liebe*. Hector seemed bemused by the name, commenting that *die alte liebe* does not mean an old love that has faded with time and gone stale; but rather a love that belongs to one's past; an old lost love; a first love perhaps; or an unrequited love one holds in one's heart for the rest of one's days. I wondered if he was trying to tell me that I reminded him of an old love in *his* life.

Hector remained the perfect gentleman aboard the ocean liner. I had my own state-room. We met for meals and had many interesting conversations, describing our lives on opposite sides of the globe. Every evening we had champagne. I quickly became accustomed to the elation it brought on. Still he remained the epit-ome of decorum: he would see me to the cabin door and kiss my hand, murmuring, *Buenas noches, señora*. And while I realized that life was not a river of champagne, that once I began work with the children my meals would probably consist of stew and puddings eaten with my charges, still, aboard ship, I entered into the spirit of the voyage and savoured every moment. For the twelve nights on the high seas I went to bed happy. Not without pride I reflected that Hector must have wanted my services badly to go to so much expense and trouble. Long before our boat docked, I knew I had fallen in love with him. Perhaps, even, I dared to hope, I would be his old love renewed.

Dear Reader, even though I subsequently mastered four languages, there are no words in any language to describe what transpired next. A taxi at the docks took us through the city. We drove along a tree-lined avenue, stopped before wrought-iron gates held open by two big men, went in along a circular drive. We drew up before a brightly lit mansion. Hector held my arm as we went up broad stone steps. Heavy, dark wooden doors swung open. I found myself in a vast marble foyer under a huge crystal chandelier. And as I stood there beside Hector, five young blonde women rushed up and hugged and kissed him, all shouting at once. Were these his little girls? And coming down the winding marble staircase was a man in a black cape, lined in red satin, then another man, and another...all in evening dress, with black patent pumps.

The woman looked up from the newspaper, tears in her eyes.

– Oh that murderer...

– You think he will kill her...?

– No, no. Have you forgotten already? In Yiddish a man who kills your feelings is the same as a murderer. Isn't that right? You murder me if you kill my feelings.

– The death of illusion, I ventured.

She ignored me. She continued the story.

Dear Reader, sitting in the comfort of your home, in the bosom of your family, reading this — Dear Reader, by now you will have guessed what had befallen me. This fine gentleman, this fatherly Hector, this model of propriety, was a white slaver! Yes, he was indeed an importer — of blonde women for his brothel! And I, who had escaped one kind of slavery, was to face the worst sort of enslavement. My young body, already abused by poverty and pregnancy, was to be ravaged by strangers. Oh the irony of it all! I had freed myself from a life of servitude to one man only to be trapped by love into a life of servitude to many men. My last thought before I fell into a dead faint was of my mother. When I regained consciousness, I was in a big bed, between satin sheets, completely naked. It was a large room, with fine furniture and mirrors everywhere. I ran to the door — it was locked! I pulled aside the heavy brocade drapes — the windows were barred! Not a trace of my clothes anywhere. The cupboards held unusual things, more like theatre costumes, all manner of strange objects such as saddles and whips, syringes and stethoscopes, chains and ropes. In the days to come what would I not have given to return to the familiar miseries I had run away from. How I longed for the smell of herring and kerosene. Meanwhile, that same night, unbeknownst to me, a gypsy caravan had entered the city. They were camped on an empty lot behind Hector's house.

— Go on, I begged, what happened to her, did the gypsies save her?

— That's all, the next instalment is in a week.

— Then I'll never know ...

— So come back in a week, I didn't mean what I said before ...

— I don't know where I'll be next week ...

Unlike an electric alarm, a brass bell against a door will announce not only the entrance, but also the age and disposition of a customer. I did not need to turn around to confirm that the short, crisp clang, a sound, I remembered, that rang of intimacy and demand, ushered in a child whose home was this bakery. He was a boy of about ten, soon followed by a younger boy, then a little girl of about six, each child heralded by a ring that was a clarion cry, It's me! It's me! It's me! Their mother left the cash register at the first swift opening of the door, and with each child in turn removed its little coat, then accumulated the garments across her bare arm, stroked each dark head, repeating You're wet! You're wet! You're wet! The children showed brave unconcern for having been caught in the rain. In order of seniority each child in turn pulled aside the maroon drape and disappeared. Their mother paused just long enough to say to me, before she too went on the other side of the curtain:

– Come again, we'll finish the story.

– I may never come this way again.

– Nobody stops you.

– I have to go where he is, the man I love.

– Just like her, the woman in the story.

– Not at all, I'm free to do what I want.

– You think so?

Alone in the bakery, I placed my purchases on the floor beside an old refrigerator: a painful decision, for one does not give up bread willingly. (I have deduced from Coenraad's indifference to certain domestic gestures that I have made from time to time that it goes against the grain of romantic love to bring to it the trappings of marriage. When we are together no stockings hang, no shirts drip; no water boils, no bread is buttered.)

On Spadina again, caught in the downpour, against which I did not lower my head, crossing block after block along a route taken a hundred years ago by colonial soldiers marching to Fort York. I was not interested in this street as history. Nor were the Chinese and Portuguese and West Indians, I thought, who all about me were hurrying to take shelter. Their expressions were the same as ours when we arrived on this street: a look that was empty of the past and that suffered the present. But their eyes gleamed as if reflecting the future that was visible all about them — a future of sturdy clothes and well-stocked stores and motor cars. Even in the rain I could see that what appeared to be new shops and buildings were only facades over the old: larger windows, bright tile, some stone work. I felt my past had not been erased, just covered over and given new names in other languages.

Just before Dundas Street my attention was caught by a large sign across the street, *Shopsy's*. Despite pangs of hunger, I could not bring myself to go inside. I kept walking, swallowing streams of saliva. In my time it had been a small delicatessen. I remembered Shopsy's parents. They stood at the steam table from morning to night, pale and patient, wearing long white aprons, their faces moist from the steamer. They were unfailingly benign towards children. The rear of the little narrow store opened onto a corridor that led to the lobby of the Yiddish theatre and patrons could buy sandwiches, pop and candy at intermission. Once, out of curiosity, I went through Shopsy's into a dark lobby, found the theater doors open and watched a rehearsal. No one but me, apparently, knew that the doors were kept open during rehearsals. I got to know the actors and actresses and had the honor of being sent for corned-beef sandwiches, one of which was for me as a tip. That sandwich! Elevated to Proustian heights by a Toronto poet as the "corned-beef madeleine." From that time on, all I have to do is bite into a sandwich and I am once more in the empty dark theater, the actors come onstage and I live out again the old melodramas of incestuous love, *dybbuks*, white slavery, lovers parted by a cruel fate.

More insistent than the memory of such moments of happiness was the picture of myself at the age of ten on these sidewalks in a cruel November rain such as this, searching for my mother. Ever since, I have been in the habit of going out in a cold rain and letting water and tears pour down my face. You would not think that a single incident could lead to an addiction, but if shock and fear are terrible enough, as it was that afternoon, then — given the same time of year, the same time of day, the same weather conditions, unable to find the one person my life depends on — then, for the rest of my days, I will seek to feel again that strange elation brought on by terror.

I weep now as I walk along Dundas, recalling that the landlady had red hair, broad shoulders and a pug nose; that it had to do with her husband who liked to come up to our attic room and sit on the bed with my mother after supper. One day, when I got home from school, she was waiting for me on the street side of the door, and no sooner did I put a foot on the first step than she shouted down, Go away, you and your whore mother don't live here any more! That door dominates my thoughts: I hear it slammed shut; I feel its weight against the jamb when I try to open it; I still attribute hate to a door when I find it locked against me. I wandered the streets, turning corners. It was this time of year; it was that time of day when everyone hurried indoors. I passed houses where lamps were lit and where children, I imagined, chattered and played. Soon the darkening streets became busy with fathers hurrying home from work and mothers dragging children back from somewhere. Then the streets emptied. I walked so long I came full circle. It is the law of the lost. I waited for my mother in a dark corner of the verandah. I was soaked to the skin and shivered with cold. She came home about ten o'clock and by that time my fears had turned to delirium. It was called a bad cold. For five days I lay in a fever in that dark attic room. No one came in to give me food or drink. My mother did what she could when she came home from work at night. That was on D'Arcy Street in 1935.

Here is the Art Gallery in its new magnificence in glass and stone, taking up an entire block. Broad, shallow steps lead up from the street. I climbed them obliquely, without strain. A last backward look at the old narrow houses across the street, picturing their dark, steep stairs off the kitchen, intended for servants who were expected to continue up stairs darker and steeper still to their attic rooms. At this moment I could actually smell again the dead air of attics. I hurried into the vast, carpeted foyer of the Gallery, which fulfilled its street promise of ease and refinement. A booklet on the counter told me that this luxury was mine until five o'clock. It also told me that

> One of the most beautiful aspects of the Gallery is its first home. Built in 1817 by D'Arcy Boulton, Jr., The Grange is now restored to Georgian elegance and gives the flavour of domestic life in early Toronto around 1835.

Downstairs, I removed my wet coat and my wet shoes, and pushed them across a wide counter towards a dispirited attendant. She handed me a numbered disc, and put its twin through the metal hook of a hanger for my coat. She hesitated at the sight of my sodden shoes, but eventually lifted them with the tips of her fingers and carried them, her arm extended, to a place under my coat. I took note of signs pointing to washroom and cafeteria, smoothed my black dress, fingered my pearls to check the clasp and set out to lose myself in silent rooms. I would stay here until my shoes dried, if not entirely, at least enough to take me to Elm Street later. At the prospect of having to locate, perhaps, ten or more streets called Elm, I felt a rising anger towards Coenraad for not having been at the first Elm; for the ambiguity of the botanical message; for causing me to return to this city to suffer the blows of memory. Even were I to find him in my bed at the hotel tonight, I was in no mood to be with my lover. Right now I was not the spirited, attractive woman he knows and wants.

Upstairs, people were moving through a turnstile with a speed unusual for gallery goers. They lost no time in getting to an area to the right and disappearing through an entrance marked *Restaurant*. When I reached the turnstile, the young woman towards whom plastic cards were being held up, addressed me with an urgent Here you are! You'll have to hurry, the awards are about to begin! Something in my gait caught her attention. She looked down at my stockinged feet. Was she concerned that I was about to receive an honor of some sort without shoes on? Had she said anything, I would have assured her that there was no reason for me to receive an award, unless it were for blind persistence.

With the others I moved towards the restaurant. At the sound of the amplified cadences of a prepared speech, I hung back, jostled by those whose course I was obstructing. I was hungry, yet the idea of being hectored before I got something to eat made me decide to leave the line and swerve sharply to my left. I found myself going down one of the corridors of the old Grange, into the first of the familiar galleries that have black marble archways, with gold letters of the benefactors' names overhead. Shoeless on the original pine floors, I went from canvas to canvas. They depicted worlds as remote to me today as they had been thirty years ago: blissful madonnas and suffering Christs; gloomy fields and bucolic herdsmen; nymphs and satyrs; sombre Flemish portraits, dark, dark, dark, relieved only by the white of ruffs at neck and wrist. Now, as I did then, I sought the flamboyant Marchesa Casati by Augustus John. I came upon her as upon a long-lost friend. There she was still, her dyed carrot-red hair, those dark wild eyes meeting mine, her two hands on one hip. At twelve I had hoped to grow up to become like her — independent, dramatic, seductive. I am not even close to that image — I am short, diffident, and my eyes are small, hazel, with invisible lashes. I never know what to do with my hands when I am not working. Now, as then, I thought her to be much more enticing than the overripe, rose-tinted virgins idealized by their painters.

If I knew how to paint I would carry a sketch pad. I would record sights that leave a deep impression — a mother gazing down tenderly on a mongoloid child at her breast; a legless man on his hands dancing across a stage strewn with shards of glass, his stumps in the air (I would make a point of picturing his broad shoulders and muscular arms); sightless lovers embracing at the airport, their white canes fallen to the floor. At the very least, as I sat and waved a charcoal pencil in the air, I would be respected as someone with an artistic bent. The guard would bring me a chair with a back to sit on. Yet, should I become a professional painter, I am afraid my success would endanger our love, since Coenraad and I differ fundamentally in our tastes. Our only quarrel took place over coffee in the Frick Museum in New York.

– Those women are unreal, I objected, yet you stand there hypnotized. Can't you see they're false as their wigs?

– You really lack an appreciation of beauty.

– It's those big breasts and blank faces you go for. All that flesh! As far as I'm concerned, nudes are a slut on the market.

– At least they're human, not some ugly mess of paint that you admire.

– It's obvious you have no understanding of Contemporary Art.

– And you have no background to appreciate the great masters.

– Huh! You talk about defending democracy, all the while you lust after the bow-legged chairs of dead aristocrats.

I have been standing in front of a Bonnard for some time, how long I cannot tell, lost in its colors, yet my eyes are drawn again and again to two long casement windows through which a clear, blue sky is visible. I cannot move. At the bottom of the frame on a little gold plaque I read, *Pierre Bonnard, Dining Room on the Garden, before 1933.* I absorb into myself the brilliant red and purple and orange until I can contain no more. There is a cloth the color of lilacs over the table. I eat fruit from white-stemmed golden bowls; I drink from a white pitcher. The sun, not seen directly, is reflected on the left wall in an oblong of gold. I advance into the canvas towards the windows which I intend to open to the perfume of the garden below. Suddenly I come across a wraith-like form, barely discernible in the right-hand corner beside the window. I draw back. I had not noticed her, as she has been painted into the background, her face the same reddish-brown as the wall, her figure obscured by a tall blue vase of red roses. As I stare at her, surprised she is still there, I notice that her mouth is tight with pain, and her eyes, which are averted, are slits beneath swollen lids. She is visibly distressed.

– Help! she cries in a whisper, I am a prisoner of my mad father!

I look around me, but there's no one else here. The girl and I are alone in the dining room on the garden.

– Help! You must save me. My father has kept me locked up here for two months!

My mind darts this way and that: I have never turned my back on someone in need, yet, right now, I don't want to start anything I can't finish. She is so young, barely seventeen. Still, I have been warned against taking up with strangers. I say to her,

– Tell me about it. Sometimes it helps to talk it out.

She cringes back into her niche. I realize that troubled persons are especially sensitive to professional jargon. I ask her what I can do.

– Take me with you!

That is impossible, of course; I cannot permit anyone to interfere with my purpose. I push past her and fling open the casement windows.

– Here, out this way, it's easy — put one foot over the sill, see how low it is, then the other foot, jump, and you're free!

She remains in her corner, shaking her head.

– There is nothing beyond this painted room. No sky, no trees, no garden. Oh these artists and their tricks! They deal in illusion: everything is a matter of perspective. See those pink flowers? You would imagine that you could just reach out and pluck them. Not at all. The pink flowers are two storeys below in the garden next door. It's not only what he paints in — all those green trees and the lovely blue sky — it's what he leaves out — that's part of the deception too. What you don't see is the twelve-foot stone wall around the yard. There is no gate. There is only the door to the kitchen of the *concierge* and he has been given orders ... One time I did try to escape. I jumped and landed on cement, not on a bed of flowers as I had been led to believe. I sprained my right ankle. See, it is still bandaged. I hobbled to the kitchen door, crying with pain. At the sight of me the *concierge* ran to the telephone, while his wife helped me to a chair. Later, from their conversation, I reconstructed what my father must have said — Poor child, she suffers from *petit mal*, her mother thought the sun would do her good. No, no, not my daughter, I am not so old as that, she is my niece from Canada. The villain, denying his paternity!

I move over to the table on the other side of the picture where there is an open-backed chair. I pull it forward and sit down. For an instant she comes out of the shadows to tell me not to disturb anything on the table.

– I myself am not in a position to help, I told her, but I travel a lot. Is there anyone I can contact on your behalf?

– Yes, yes, when you get to Paris, tell the Canadian Consul of my plight and persuade him to intervene with the local authorities here. I warn you, that will not be a simple matter in France. I, as a minor, have no recourse to the law against my father.

I promised. She came and sat opposite me at the table and told me her story.

– I left a harsh life in Rimouski for the glamour of the Riviera. My poor mother was on relief, I had to leave school, the Depression was getting worse and worse. My mother traced my father through relatives in the Old Country and discovered he was living in Antibes, a place, she thought, where everyone was rich, even in those times. And so I came to live with the father I had never known. I am the same age as my mother was when they ... when I was conceived. I think my father sometimes forgot who I was: he had a strange expression on his face when he looked at me. But now he looks at me only with anger, sometimes even with hatred. He won't speak to me. Worst of all, he won't let me out of this room. For my own good, he says. I have had nothing to eat for a week but dry crusts of bread; I drink coffee made with chicory. The fruit in the bowl? It is made of wax. No, there is nothing in the pitcher. It has all been created for effect. My father is penniless. I have written home for money. He says my mother will have to pay if she wants me back. I explain that my mother is on welfare. He says I am lying because everyone in America has money. Tears come to my eyes.

    – Why is he doing this to you?

    – Because I disobeyed him. Just once. Once, that's all. I had a rendezvous with a young man against my father's orders. I met Emil at a tea-dance at the Hotel Renoir. I was out for a walk, I heard the music and I went into the hotel. I was lonely and bored. Emil was alone too. We danced. He is a student from Heidelberg. My father says he is a pimp employed by the hotel to turn me into a whore like my mother. Or else he is a German spy. He says the Germans are everywhere. It's true, but only as tourists. I promised Emil I would come to the hotel the next afternoon. My father forbade me to go, but I went out just the same. I am accustomed to being on my own, with my mother away looking for work most of the day. You must believe me — my father will not — that we were never alone, Emil and I. We talked and drank lemonade and danced. I went right home when the dance was over. It was only six o'clock, but still my father was enraged. There was a terrible scene. Like mother, like daughter, he kept saying. The next morning a doctor came. I can't imagine what he was told. The doctor tried to get me to lie down and spread my legs. I refused. Then he and my father tried to force me to submit to an examination, but I fought them both. Finally, while my father held me, the doctor put a square of wet gauze over my face. When I woke up, the doctor was gone. I was nauseated and sore all over, but otherwise unharmed. I am to stay in this room, my father says, until money arrives from my mother; or until he finds someone willing to pay a handsome price for my virginal favors, whichever happens first.

– The world has changed, I suggested. Young women are no longer at the mercy of men.

– What you say may be true, but that does not free me from my father.

– I know someone who is employed by the American government. I'll get him to use his influence with the Ambassador in Paris.

– It's no use, she whispered, I'm just a young girl. They will take his word against mine. Then she retreated quickly to her corner and faded back into the wall.

In Paris, I was so caught up with waiting each day for Coenraad's arrival, so obsessed with thoughts of the joy awaiting me, each morning recalling the delirium of the night before; the next night waiting for his return, waiting for the knock on the door, waiting for his entry ... that I forgot about the girl in Antibes. Not until it was too late, when the American Embassy had to be barricaded against rioting students in '67, and Coenraad got a message to me to leave immediately and I was on a plane to London, did I remember my promise.

I hoped she got away from her father and out of France before it fell. In the light of subsequent events, the rise of Nazism, the war, the defeat of France, I wondered about Emil. Was he who he said he was? I will never know. I wept all day, every day. The doctor came again and said I was very ill. He, my father, would be well advised to send me back to Canada. While they regarded one another very seriously, I found my voice.

– You've had your revenge, you've made my mother pay, you've punished me, no more, no more, let me go . . .

I thought I heard her cry out. Someone cried out. It was a long-drawn-out cry of despair one hears at the graveside. I looked about and saw two policemen coming towards me. Perhaps it was not too late to appeal to the law. In the midst of my recounting to them her tragic story, they exchanged conspiratorial glances; they looked at one another every few seconds as if to reassure themselves that they had both, at the same time, seen and heard the identical thing. With one accord they moved from a position facing me to stand one on either side. I saw determination on their faces. I saw also that their uniforms were brown. I heard something about a doctor. A cold was numbing my limbs; I could not move. Not until they took hold of my arms with unexpected gentleness did I realize they were gallery guards.

– I get these attacks, I spoke slowly and distinctly, as one does in a foreign country, *petit mal*, I'll be all right in a few minutes, thank you, and declined further help with a firm step backward. Coenraad, had he been with me, would have applauded my inventiveness. I would have nudged him to pay particular attention to the sincerity with which I lied my way out of an embarrassment: the way I looked the guards straight in the eye and the way I placed a hand on the shoulder of the shorter one. Coenraad has said that my inability to dissimulate is more of a vice than a virtue; that I hold nothing back; that there is no mystery about me whatsoever. It isn't as if life for me has been a mere matter of honesty, to paraphrase Virginia Woolf. She also said that candor is the greatest vice. It seems to me that in a confusion of extremes one either lies or tells the truth, whichever works best. Up until now the risk of deceit has, for me, been greater than the risk of truth.

With thoughts of Coenraad again as pervasive as a fever I returned directly to the King Edward. In this mood there is always a feeling that by sheer concentration I can conjure up my lover. As I pushed against the heavy glass of the revolving door I tamed an impulse once inside to run across the lobby to the desk and demand my message. It has been my experience that eagerness born of anxiety sets up a perversity in clerks, so that without as much as a turn of the head or a shift of the eyes, they will say *No*. I have tried a brisk step with an air intended to suggest the snapping of fingers, but I fool no one: I simply do not command the respect of those paid to serve. I am forced to see myself through their eyes: a woman, no longer young, in a tweed coat open over a plain black dress. A closer look would reveal only that the pearls around my throat are genuine. Since I am a middle-aged woman travelling alone, I cannot be identified by the company I keep. I carry one small suitcase; there is not even a briefcase to give me a little prestige. I am regarded as a woman with no apparent purpose, offering no reason for my presence. When I leave, everyone's attitude changes: they smile as I pay the bill; another clerk voluntarily checks to see if there is a final message. Even the ubiquitous fat detective with the fat cigar nods goodbye from his position in the big chair. Their fears are ended. I have caused no disturbance. I am not insane; no men were seen leaving my room in the middle of the night; no vengeful husband has stormed in; the police have made no enquiries. With a split-second timing I always wonder at, my bag is placed in the front seat beside the driver in a waiting cab. I have no alternative but to get into the taxi and state my destination.

But right now I had to make the arduous journey across the expanse of carpet in the lobby of the King Edward. My shoes were still wet and uncomfortable. I began to limp. The clerks and the tired old men dressed as busboys, and some botanists heading for the Bacchus Bar at the other end, all watched with sympathy. I dragged my left leg towards the desk. When the odds are against me I go into an act. See, I'm crippled, I haven't had your advantages; it's been rough, but what can you know about it. I got the idea at a concert. A famous soprano came onstage, emerging slowly from the wings, pathetically dragging her lame leg behind her, and as we followed her painful path to centre stage, we were not only without criticism but we had our palms together ready to applaud before she opened her mouth. By the time I reached the desk, the clerk was truly sorry he had no message for me. He wished me a pleasant evening. I limped to the elevators. In my room I stayed just long enough to change into my other pair of shoes. Downstairs again, I was careful to remember to limp back across the lobby. A busboy ran forward to start the doors revolving slowly for me.

On Yonge Street I found myself part of an indeterminate crowd. They will, I know, finally go into Simpson's or Eaton's or Woolworth's for something to do. I stayed on the east side of the street in order to avoid the same temptation. I crossed only after I got to Elm Street, although I did linger in front of Loew's Downtown to look at the stills of movie stars about to make love. At the corner of Dundas a sudden chill wind came up. The United Clothiers showed overcoats and parkas in their window.

When I turned the corner on Elm Street I found that where Number Four might have been there was a patch of dying grass and a green park bench. Number Forty, then, became my destination, but as I looked up the street I saw only devastation. Except for a couple of magnificent old brick buildings, four storeys high, the entire centre of Elm Street had been wrecked. What was left habitable were a few small restaurants, houses with renovated fronts with signs proclaiming they were clubs — Order of the

Eagles, Orange Order, Order of Serbian Veterans, Order of Elks, Order of Croatian Veterans — and parking lots, the backs of the Mount Sinai Hospital and the Sick Children's Hospital. I passed old homes boarded up, awaiting, I presumed, demolition. What type of disguise would Coenraad find suitable for this mongrel street? As I walked along, the street lamps came on. The white light of the sodium vapor lamps created stark shadows. Few people were about. A young girl about twelve passed me and I began to ruminate on *Innocence and Its Loss.*

This is the type of essay I write in my head and save up to tell Coenraad. I can't very well talk about Innocence and Its Loss with the bellhop. It isn't that I automatically assume that a bellhop is incapable of metaphysical insights. "I've seen everything" is also a statement of profundity. It's just that I do not want to start something I cannot finish. No sooner do I get a dialogue under way than I have to leave. Suppose he is troubled by his place in the scheme of things, as I am by mine; and I come along and, with the best intentions in the world, probe his soul with stiletto questions, such as, How long have you been a bellhop? and he, at age forty-seven, begins to consider his existential dilemma and he ceases to be content with being a bellhop — is it my fault that he quits, goes on unemployment insurance, doesn't know how to begin a day on his own, takes to drink — am I responsible for his fate?

Yet, even though on abstract issues Coenraad is, I feel, an original thinker, I am reluctant to involve his intellect when we are together. Once I queried him on the phenomenological aspects of his work — all that spying and interrogation; all those disguises and mysteries; all that moving about from country to country; all those ploys and stratagems — is he satisfied to go on this way?

– Love me, he said, ask no questions. Coenraad always eludes my probings.

I stepped up on the porch of Number Forty. It was perhaps the last house remaining on Elm Street. On my left was a large window, we used to call it the front-room window, with a round green sign glued to the corner nearest the steps. The imprint said, *Metro Toronto Licensed Boarding House.* There was a bell but I hesitated to use it. Whom would I ask for? I have no way of describing Coenraad, except, perhaps, as a single man, recently arrived in Toronto. In a city this size, I realized, the description would apply to thousands of men. The door, I noticed, was within an inch of being shut; it yielded to pressure. I found myself in a dark hall. Dark, because no one, not the landlady nor any tenant, would replace the burnt-out 40-watt bulb. Dark, too, because every door was shut tight by the occupants, even though, I recalled, they have nothing to hide, neither goods nor dignity. Yet they insist on privacy. At this hour, there were smells of frying lard mixed with odors of old dust and with those strange emanations of skin and breath and cloth, still lingering, of countless people who have come and gone in this hall.

As I stood there in the dark I was assailed by doubt. Where in this tenement would I find Coenraad? There were three storeys and perhaps even a basement of rooms. Someone brushed against me and for a moment my heart leapt. But he (it was) opened the door into the room to the right of where I was standing. The smell of beer on his breath confirmed he could not be Coenraad, who never drinks, on or off duty. He left the door ajar: I had only to turn my head to see inside, but that was not necessary. I know this type of "light-housekeeping" room very well, with its two-burner electric plate; with its battered brown studio couch that opens into a bed and a half; with its tall, dark, veneered, double-doored wardrobe. One door has a cracked mirror; the other door holds a small key in its broken lock and is always open unless a wedge of newspaper between it and the frame keeps it shut. When the door is opened the wad of paper falls to the floor and is not replaced, so that entire weeks are spent staring at the worn shoes and old coats inside. There is also a small radio sitting on the table beside the toaster.

Through the open doorway I could hear the television. Then over the electronic voices I heard real shouts, then a crash and a woman's (real) scream. Such sounds are not unfamiliar to me and I listened for the sequence I knew to be inevitable. First, a scraping sound. I imagined she has pulled forward a wooden chair which she holds an inch or so off the floor, ready to swing it either for protection or for assault. I visualized her strong, heavy arms. Then I heard her voice, rich with rage, Get away from me you drunken bastard the next time you're late you can take your own goddam supper stay away I'm warning you don't you dare touch me . . . And he, I'll come home any fuckin time I want I'm your husband I'll clobber you if you don't put that fuckin chair down . . .

By holding up my wrist to the gleam of light from the doorway, I saw that it was only six-thirty. At first I was puzzled by the woman's complaint — after all, only children eat dinner before seven — until I recalled the fried herring and the potatoes and the urgings to "finish already." Someone would always say, I'm too tired to eat. It would have been barely six o'clock. When the table was cleared, it would have been understood that the final obligation of the day had been discharged by everyone. There would be released in us then a surge of freedom — the remaining hours belonged to each of us alone. The house would quiet down. The door to the street would open and close discreetly.

The television voice was clicked off in midsentence. I heard the man speak in low, insinuating tones; then the woman's in reply, soft now; and, finally, their door being (kicked?) shut. For several moments I stood there in the dark and breathed in the smells of the poor, thinking that Coenraad, were he with me now, would take my hand and pull me out of this place, exactly as he did that time when our rendezvous turned out to be a hovel of a hotel in Manchester. He has an aversion, which I do not share, to poverty. Coenraad refuses to reveal whether, like me, he once was very poor or whether he has never known deprivation. I agree that in his line of work, with days and nights fraught with danger, he needs to be able to count on something. He can count on me; I think he knows that; I could love him anywhere. And yet . . . I am always drawn back to poverty. I am aware that there are a dozen streets named Elm, in the suburbs, in Rosedale, in North York, still, on my first day back, I sought the shabby streets of my youth. Suddenly what I thought was self-evident in the message now appeared vague and uncertain: Did I really expect to find Coenraad here?

Despite the disintegration of the street, I came across an elegant restaurant. It, too, was boarded up, except that its blind exterior suggested exclusiveness. The front was of dark, burnished wood, reflecting pale yellow lights; dashes of color were provided by stained glass windows. From where I stood on the sidewalk nothing could be seen of its interior. Some couples, well-dressed, strong perfume on the women, passed me and went inside. Even then as the door was opened I could see nothing. To the left of the door was a menu under glass. The food and the prices, I thought, indicated a clientele I could be part of if I wanted to: I would fit right in with my good black dress and the pearls; I know how to order in French; how to use a knife and fork in the English manner; how to place without ostentation my credit card on the little silver tray with the bill. But right now, I wanted to cling to what the day had evoked: the encounter in the bakery, the tears in the rain, the shock of the Bonnard, the smells of the boarding house.

On Yonge Street, between Elm and Dundas, I saw a sign in angular letters, *Naxos*. It was repeated on a door to the left of a shoe shop. Stairs led up to a small, bright restaurant. The waitress and I were the only women in a roomful of men. Most had come from work, to judge by their clothes. Were their wives still in the Old Country? I was led to a small table, which was vacated at my approach by two men who had been only sitting and smoking. This was done wordlessly. An ashtray was removed and the plastic over a red-checkered cloth was wiped clean. Yet, even here, in this plain room with bare windows, aspirations were evident. The menu, found behind the cash register, was elaborately printed. Although the dishes had Greek names, the headings were set in Old English type: *Ye Starte*, and, for the desserts, *Ye Finish*. The owner came around the counter to bid me welcome and to urge me to come again and bring my friends, then went back to watch over my shish kebab at the broiler. A jukebox pounded Greek music. Eventually it became silent and no one put in any more coins. In a corner, two tables over, four men sipped Turkish coffee and smoked steadily. I took them to be intellectuals from the way they held their cigarettes between thumb and forefinger and from the fact that they wore jackets, shirts and ties. Their hushed tones and their occasional outbursts made me think they were talking about the military *coup* in Greece. It was in my mind to go over and ask them a question that had been nagging me. In the knowledge, though, of torture and repression in that country I was afraid my words would not be taken at their simple value; perhaps they would be suspicious of my intrusion, looking upon it as a feminine ploy to gain access to their politics or their sex. I wanted to ask them if they knew why Theseus abandoned Ariadne on the island of Naxos. Did Theseus abandon Ariadne because he no longer loved her; or, as one legend claimed, because his ship was blown out to sea? . . .

At nine o'clock that night I went again, as I had in the morning, against the flow. Everyone hurried north as they came out of the Queen Street subway, hurrying, I imagined, to catch the last show or the remaining hours in a bar. Only four of us crossed the street in the opposite direction. At King Street an elderly man waited with me for the lights to change. He kept his eyes on the ground, yet, as the light turned green, I was aware he was keeping pace with me. I turned the corner slowly towards the hotel, but he continued to shuffle south. I was the only person left on the street.

Through the revolving doors, through the lobby again as if crippled, being careful to bend the right knee as before, establishing almost a dance rhythm. It is evident that I have given myself a handicap, in the sporting sense. The night clerk watched my progress towards him. He made a concession, a minor one perhaps, but important to me: his information was given in a complete sentence.

– I am very sorry, madame, but there is nothing in your box tonight; maybe there will be a message for you tomorrow. Have a good evening.

In what way, I wondered.

Then I caught sight of a group of botanists. There were seven to be exact, four men and three women, still wearing their tags. They stood in the exact centre of the lobby, under the huge chandelier, an earnest congregation in dark suits and black shoes and in dresses in small print. I felt impelled to join them: I had to find out who, amongst the delegates, left the botany journal and the message of diseased elms. It was possible that the extra man, the one without a partner, was Coenraad. But which one? I gathered, from stray words reaching me, they were trying to decide what to do with the rest of the night. I hung about in the hope that one of them was my lover.

It was not possible to assess the mating combinations, not in their faces, which were one and at the same time impersonal and yet animated; not in the way they stood, which was one and at the same time far apart and yet close together. I sought the eyes of each of the men in turn. When Coenraad has no other safe means of communication, he signals me with a deep look into my eyes, blinking three times between unwavering stares. The hawk-headed one with the bushy brows and a gray plume of hair avoided my gaze; another, whose heavy-lidded eyes looked back at me with melancholy, was having his maroon knitted tie straightened by one of the women; the eyes of the third one were crinkled with laughter as he chuckled ho-ho-ho's; the last stood four-square in Roots boots and met my gaze, although not in that special transfixed stare. He had red hair, his face was shaven down to the fringe of a lighter red beard tracing the jawline in Mennonite fashion. That's the sort of disguise Coenraad prefers, a readily identifiable type, easily recalled by a witness in a description to the police. I stepped forward and said evenly,

– Is there any hope for the elm?

– A chemical compound has been developed, the Mennonite replied, that can be injected into the base of an elm tree to inhibit the progress of the disease.

The new code was working! I have been persuaded never to tip my hand, as the expression goes, when we meet in public. I therefore maintained an air of neutrality and awaited further signals. The Mennonite was saying that he for one wished to go to bed now, it had been a long day; moreover, he, for one again, was not interested in a nightclub with topless waitresses, although as a scientist he'd be the first to acknowledge the usefulness of the female breast for the survival of the human race. Up to now, that is. How like him to make reference to breasts, knowing I would recall the nights he lay beside me quoting from the Song of Songs, *Thy two breasts are like two young roes that are twins which feed among the lilies.* I said I had to prepare my paper on *Ceratocystis ulmi.*

Perhaps they attributed my announcement to embarrassment, because I was blushing with memory and anticipation. The Mennonite recognized the Latin term for the blight that has destroyed the magnificent elms. I'd like to have a copy of your paper, he told me. I could barely contain my joy. On my way to the elevators I slowed down my lame steps to give Coenraad, if indeed it was he, a chance to catch up with me. Just as I entered the elevator, all seven of them came in. They were laughing, the men poked one another with their elbows, the women stood with lowered eyes. I concluded that the mere idea of voyeurism had been sufficient for their evening's excitement. Five of them, including the Mennonite, got out on the eighth floor, without a backward glance. The other two got out on the ninth.

It was with reluctance that I turned the key in the door to my room: I dreaded the sight of the plastic surfaces and the bilious colors, in the midst of which I would have to endure the long night ahead. Nor, once inside, could I bring myself to secure the bolts and chains provided for my safety: a sealed door right now would end all hope that Coenraad would come through it: I had to be able to open it quickly with just a twist of the knob. I pressed my back against the door as if to postpone my entry into the room proper, which, despite the many pieces of furniture and the television set on its own stand, and the lamps that lit up with a switch in the hallway — that room despite efforts to appear crowded with amenities, was empty.

A light tap on the door behind my back caused my spine to reverberate as though there'd been an explosion outside. I controlled an impulse to fling open the door — it might be one of those hotel spies sent out in the late evening with a towel over the arm, who makes her slow way to the bathroom, all the while darting quick searching glances into every corner. I opened the door, not too wide, and remained hidden behind it, as they do in the movies, so that if it were Coenraad he would be forced to pay a small penalty, as is exacted by children in their games, for having kept me in suspense the past twenty-four hours. I pictured him on the other side, hesitating, not knowing whether it was his lover or his enemy on the inside. Or perhaps it was really I who was afraid to risk knowing whether it was my lover or a rapist who was demanding entrance. There was no retreat. It was necessary to dissipate the charge being created by the two of us.

I confronted a black man in beige overalls. A broad leather belt was around his waist. Attached to the belt was a pouch full of tools, the weight of which caused the belt to hang low over his hip. He was leaning against the door frame, with a patient look. He said he had come to repair the telephone. I said it did not need fixing. He asked me how I knew that, having just come in. I asked how did he know *that*? During this exchange I speculated that if he were Coenraad, and he were being watched, he had to "play it straight" until I, the occupant, let him in. But, reluctantly, I had to face the fact that his height was exceptional; his head almost touched the top of the door frame. Coenraad can disguise almost everything, even his color, but not his height. That is to say, he can by means of platforms on his shoes extend himself to about five foot eleven, but unless he were on stilts, he could never measure, as did the man before me, several inches over six feet. He was now regarding me with an air of here-we-go-again, as in all those crime shows on television, where the assassin pretends he is a telephone repair man. I concealed my eyes, because he read in them the memories of countless crime shows I have watched in countless hotel rooms, dramas wherein the murderer gains access to his victim by pretending to be a telephone repair man. I blocked the doorway.

– There is no need to repair it. I never telephone anyone.

I watched him go down the hall and waited until he turned a corner before I came back into my room. He may have been a rapist, a killer, a thief, but I could not have brought myself to shut the door in his face.

I tried the phone. It was dead. I felt ashamed of my suspicions. I told myself that so much caution had led to uncertainty, which had led to distrust. As recently as a year ago I was still flinging open the door to any signal — a tap, a rap, a ring. In Quito one morning last March, I responded to light taps and the sound of heavy breathing. An intense little man fell at my feet, exhausted. I, assuming it was Coenraad, gathered him in my arms and pulled him inside the hotel room. When he shrank from my affections, doubt assailed me. Up to then all our meetings from Mexico to Belize to Ecuador had gone smoothly. Quickly I checked our code in the *National Geographic* and found nothing to account for the terrified, ragged, emaciated figure pleading wordlessly for sanctuary. Just then, a key in the lock and the maid slipped in, pushing the cleaning cart ahead of her. There were muffled cries and embraces. I helped her lift him into the canvas laundry container and we covered him with towels. At that hour, eleven in the morning, no one was in the corridor except another maid at the far end. I walked ahead of the cart in case someone appeared who needed to be diverted. The maid gave me a grateful, anguished smile as the door to the service elevator clattered shut on her and her cargo. When I told Coenraad about my adventure, he assumed I had been badly frightened and he attempted to reassure me: the terrorist's presence in our room was sheer coincidence. The maid was his wife. Besides, he added, they had both been apprehended in the laundry in the basement.

That same hot afternoon with Coenraad beside me in a darkened room, I forgot everything; that same night when we strolled the streets under a navy-blue sky, no thought came to me of what would be done with the two prisoners; later that same night, drinking rum and listening to itinerant singers confessing love in falsetto voices, plucking at their guitars in despair, I never once thought of torture; and back in that same room, after quiet prolonged lovemaking falling into a dreamless sleep at dawn, it never occurred to me that those other two would never wake to another day.

On the plane to Guatemala I reflected on the nature of coincidence. Was it pure bad luck that brought the guerilla leader (his picture was on the front page at the newsstands) to seek safety in Coenraad's room; was it fate that his wife was a maid in that room; was it mere chance that an ally, myself, was the mistress of the very man who had been ordered to capture him? . . . I was assailed again by that unholy trinity of doubt, distrust and suspicion. Was Coenraad using me in his work, was his love affair just another cover? It's just as well the telephone is out of order: there is danger in its use with my overwrought imagination. Except for that one call in Tikal, Coenraad and I have never spoken on the telephone because of wire taps. Telephones are ringing behind every wall, but I receive no calls nor do I dare make any. (In the letter to my children I will draw attention to the fact that the telephone is theirs exclusively from now on. Their father is satisfied to receive a mid-week report on Wednesday night on his mare at the stables, otherwise he rarely finds use for the apparatus. Just think, my dear ones, you will not have to wonder for whom the bell rings: it will ring for you. I made all those allusions to this-is-your-home, yet you never felt the phone belonged to you. It's all yours now. That is what I will write.)

I sat on the edge of the bed and contemplated the useless instrument on the night table. It was colored beige and had a two-inch-wide drawer that pulled out of its bottom, with tiny plastic-covered pages that gave instructions for its use for various hotel services, for local and long-distance calls. There were also advertisements and numbers for a taxi, a nightclub, an escort service, restaurants of exotic ethnicity. I reflected that within its deceptively simple design the telephone contains at any given moment such portents of joy or disaster, of boredom or terror, that even a shaman would fall in a faint with fear of the spirits that come shrieking through its wires. It is just as well I cannot use the phone: I might be tempted to look up the number of someone I once knew. What would I say after all these years?

– Hello, is this Maximilian's mother? This is — this was — Shirley Silverberg. Listen. I must ask you something. If you had not sent your son away and he would have taken me dancing a few more times and I had put my face on his chest against that silky white shirt I know you ironed for him to go out in, and he would have been careful to keep his hand around my waist while we danced and when the music stopped lead me to our table, and when they played *The Last Waltz* he would have kissed me lightly on the cheek (did you imagine we ever did more than kiss?); if I had only been able to calmly announce to my father some Saturday night that I was going to the movies and Max drove up in his father's Buick (instead, I often muttered a bitter "nowhere" when my father demanded to know where I'd been); if Max and I had had a few phone calls in the spring when he was writing exams and I told him I was promoted from stenographer to secretary, and anyway I had to wash my hair and catch up on my reading, had he ever read Bernanos?; if, in early summer, after his exams, he picked me up at Herbert House after work and we walked down to the lake and spent our exuberance in the icy waters kicking and splashing each other, gasping for breath; and if, afterwards, making certain no one was about, and no one ever was at that time of year, kissed long and longingly; if you had taken some one else to lunch and left us to make certain discoveries — his imperious manner, my bluntness, his oily hair, my shoes that pinched, his sudden silences, my outbursts on streetcars — then in time we would have telephoned one another less often and, finally, perhaps, stopped seeing each other altogether. If you had left us alone then Maximilian need not have broken his back and I need not have married a man who reminded me of him.

Zbigniew. The fault was not his. He happened to have eyes set deep under a straight brow; he happened to have a small waist below the hollows under his ribs; and his buttocks were small and muscular; his fingers were long and his feet narrow. He happened to have those features I had to reclaim as mine.

Zbigniew has done nothing wrong. He never breathes in my face. The fault is not his that I cannot look into his unclouded eyes, that I cannot meet the gaze that once commanded a squadron. I am afraid of hands (his) that exert an iron control over horses. For a long time now I have not raised my voice. Any agitation on my part brings to the bedroom two men in white. The ambulance lights flash; the crowd gathers; the siren splits the air; Zbigniew receives sympathy.

No, the fault is not my husband's that I am sitting on the edge of a bed in a hotel room, alone, staring at a dead telephone.

The day having been uneventful, time spent unrequited and my hopes unfulfilled, I got to bed as quickly as possible. I flipped the postcards with the desperation of an addict. The colors flashed: castles and gardens, bridges and statues, museums and market-places. All, all, bringing to mind scenes more vivid, more graphic in detail, than the actual event through which I had passed with all my senses reeling. Only in retrospect do I hear the peal of church bells, smell the food in the stalls, hear the words of our murmurings in the dark, recognize the sources of our laughter. Even the silences are felt again in their exact meaning. Coenraad was right: it is with memories like these that pleasures are restored. Once, in

Venice, in a gondola within sight of the Bridge of Sighs, I looked up at the little grilles through which the condemned on their way to their dark, dank prisons had their last sight of the Venetians. I wept for all who have had to relinquish the little they have known of happiness.

– Now what's wrong?

– Each time we are together I think it may be for the last time. He tried to comfort me.

– Happiness, he said, is memories.

Reveries of happiness began to give way to other images, more importunate. That same night in Venice, I, or at any rate, my Canadian passport, was instrumental in saving Coenraad from the law. It wasn't the first time, nor was it to be the last. That night we were recumbent on pillows in a gondola. It was May 11, and it was my forty-second birthday. The gondolier was singing *La Donna è Mobile*, his oar dipped rhythmically and he pretended to be watching the canal traffic ahead. I opened my eyes now and then to view the crescent moon behind Coenraad's head. We were just about to pass under the Rialto bridge when the gondolier hissed, Quickly, *signor*, it is the police, and he and Coenraad exchanged jackets and places. When the police motorboat pulled alongside they shone a flashlight into the gondolier's face. I found my passport and held up its blue cover to the light, while the gondolier smirked and spoke rapidly, removing his arms from my waist to gesticulate wildly, and the four policemen smiled and shrugged. After they pulled away, Coenraad said something in Italian. Somehow, he and the gondolier seemed to share a tacit knowledge, for he, the gondolier, once more embraced me. Coenraad plied the oar; he didn't attempt to sing; we rocked on the water; I didn't attempt to extricate myself from the man's hard grasp.

Again it was my Canadian passport that saved Coenraad. After Venice, we met in the Paul Cezanne Hotel in Aix-en-Provence.

Every morning Coenraad took the first train to Marseilles, returning every night after midnight. He asked if Paul Cezanne suspected anything. He must have been joking. Because he had spent so little time with me in Aix, Coenraad, as a gesture of conciliation, permitted me to travel with him on the train to Paris. We had a private compartment on the Trans-Europe-Express. At Lyons two plainclothesmen burst in on us. They demanded that we show passports and open suitcases. I held up my passport with CANADA in gold print close to the eyes of one and then the other.

– Ah, Canada! affably, adding he was pleased that de Gaulle had visited Quebec. And you, *monsieur*?

To my surprise, Coenraad extracted from an inner pocket of his jacket on a hook opposite a document in the same dark blue color. One of the detectives had a thick soft-covered book under his arm which he consulted after writing down the numbers of our passports. Lewd looks all around. I interpreted these to mean that in our state of undress they took us to be a couple of Canadians in France having an illicit rendezvous. They were half right.

In the King Edward at this hour of the night every room seems sealed off: no footsteps in the corridor, no doors banging shut. Outside, the city's tumult is stilled. In certain sleepless states I have apprehensions of doom; my heart pumps furiously, even though I lie perfectly still. I attribute this to a fear my body knows, a fear my mind cannot name. Don't be afraid, I chide myself, you have not been abandoned; Coenraad has been delayed, that's all. Trust yourself, trust him, he loves you. Remember how he loves you. Gradually my heart slows down. I turn over on my left side. Sleep will not come: thoughts, vague and discontinuous, fill the darkness. Out of the flow, one idea obtrudes: some snow fell today. Gradually the significance of the weather strikes me. I am forced to contrast our meetings in cold climates with those in warm zones. In countries around the equator our love is at its hottest. Trade winds and warm waters, torpor in the day and ardor in the night. The heat keeps us in a fever of desire. Everything we eat is spiced with aphrodisiacs. We have never had harsh words in São Paulo or Rangoon or Palermo. Nor do we speak of matters that might cast a shadow across our sun: about hungry men, dying women, disfigured children; about arrests at night and executions at dawn. Later, I will read about such things in airports. But in the midst of it all, we know only one another in complete felicity. Coenraad jokes with policemen carrying submachine guns. In the colder regions something goes wrong. Whatever the cause — the cold or the damp or the gray pall — we quarrel easily. I must choose my words with care, ask no questions, avoid witticisms. (Amsterdam was an exception. Perhaps Coenraad felt at ease in his ancestral home. Perhaps being below sea level has something to do with an atavistic desire to return to water. The three nights we had at the Hotel Krasnapolski were spent in calm embraces and long sleeps, as if collapse of the dikes was imminent. And should we be washed away, we would be found clutching one another in our eternal repose.) In Stockholm, he was so easily irked and I so quickly wounded, that he sent me on to Edinburgh ahead of schedule. Despite a week's separation, the coolness between us persisted. Coenraad had no enthusiasm for anything; he refused to visit the Castle with me. North of the forty-second parallel we always fuck without passion.

In Hamburg our affair almost came to an end.

I had taken a long walk beside the Elbe. It was a cold, damp day in March and by four o'clock I was glad to be inside the hotel. In Germany, inevitably, I suffered from a rampant imagination. I was grateful, therefore, that Coenraad's message had brought me to Vier Jahreszeiten, where the splendour clung to the nineteenth century. In the lounge a fire was crackling in the huge hearth, its flames fitfully reflected on the gleaming oak walls. Everything shone: crystal and silver and polished leather chairs. On a long table at one end copper chafing dishes were set out on a white damask cloth. A chef in a high white hat was whipping a sauce in a copper bowl; to his right an assistant handed him a spatula, wooden handle forward as a nurse hands an instrument to a surgeon. Waiters in black suits glided about the room, starched white aprons tied at their waists and flapping at their ankles above polished black shoes. I sat at a small table. Two waiters came at once. I ordered coffee and cake. A third waiter appeared, murmured, *Bitte*?, pulled out the other chair and helped a woman sit opposite me. She addressed me in accented English, Ah, you are here. So. And began to pull off long white kid gloves. She was stout, yet elegant in a black velvet suit with a white satin blouse. She leaned her elbows and her breasts on the table, rested her (hennaed) head in her hands and began, quietly, to weep. Her fingers were covered with rings: two diamond, one broad gold band, one ruby, an emerald and a turquoise. Coffee and small cakes were brought. She sipped and nibbled and wept. Although I have been warned never to speak to strangers, my heart went out to this pathetic person.

– You mustn't cry in public, I told her.

– It's the only safe place to cry.

– You humiliate yourself and embarrass others.

– You believe that because you are in love. Yes, yes, I can tell. It is difficult for one in love to think of tears. If one is given to weeping as I am, it is easier to cry in the company of one who is happy.

I was still drinking my first cup of coffee when yet another waiter brought me a second. I was about to dismiss him and his coffee when he began to remove from a silver tray and place before me silver pitchers of cream, one after the other, seven of them. It was a signal! To make certain, I looked down at his shoes. They were not black and pointed like the others. He was wearing a pair of brown brogues. I looked up into a pair of gray warning eyes.

– I wasn't always like this, she was saying. It started with a little sniffle before dinner, then a few tears as a nightcap. As the empty days dragged on, I got into the habit of feeling sorry for myself in the middle of the afternoon. Before I knew it, I was having out-bursts before breakfast. I forgot to eat: I cried instead. My health suffered. I became thin, nervous, unable to control my craving for that blessed release of warm, salt tears. My dear, may that day never come for you when you cannot control your tears. I am not so bad now. I am able to hold out until four in the afternoon when my chauffeur brings me here for tea. Everyone is so kind. I am not alone; people try to help. Often I am joined by someone ready to give way and shed a few tears with me. You would be surprised how many people, from every part of the world, have pent-up sorrows and need only a little encouragement to let go.

She proferred a fine lawn handkerchief, folded, with "E" embroidered in pink silk in the corner.

– No thank you, I have no tears left.

– You poor dear, it must have been dreadful.

– Actually, it never occurred to me to come out in the open. I cried in the basement, in the dark, so no one would know. Often I did my laundry at the same time.

Her eyes brimmed over, then she covered her face with the (now-unfolded) hanky and began to sob. My waiter hovered. I poured the seven creams into my empty cup, met his glare and said, That will be all, thank you.

None of this byplay diverted the woman opposite me, who, as the expression goes, was well into her cups.

– My husband will be released from prison next week, she was saying. He has bleeding ulcers, I will have to cook milk soups for him. What do I want with him now? Everything has gone on as if he were dead. The factories are humming, the servants run the house. Once I cried because he left me alone; now I cry because he is coming back. What will I do with him wandering about the house, getting in everyone's way? . . . And every evening we will make our promenade around the grounds for an hour, in every sort of weather, in rain and snow.

– Leave, go far away, it's not too late!

– Ah, the young, they know what they must do. For me it is too late. Too late to sleep in strange beds. I have gone through so much. Two world wars, many changes, my friends dead, my son in Argentina, my daughters in America, my husband in prison . . .

– Your husband is a Nazi!

– Never. He owned factories; he did what he was told.

– You were his wife, you should have stopped him!

– He was my husband, he did not consult me whether he should produce tanks.

Sadly I nodded in understanding: Zbigniew spends all his spare hours with his mare; Coenraad (what exactly is his work?) will not juggle one assignment for an extra night with me.

– Sell your jewels, pack your hankies, go! You have learned to cry amidst strangers; you can live anywhere!

It was beyond my comprehension why I would want to comfort this fat old woman whose very existence was a sign of guilt, a woman who no doubt drank champagne in her private bunker while my family . . . gone . . . all gone . . . I am the only one left alive. My own tears began to flow. I accepted, unfolded and used the handkerchief she handed me. I kept crying, quietly, naturally, relieved to know I still had tears in me. At the very least, I could weep for the dead. The woman was dry-eyed now. Sober, one might say.

– No, my dear, forgive me, she was saying, you have been so kind, but I cannot exchange boredom for danger. I have suffered enough. Now I have my little pleasures every day at four o'clock to look forward to. You will agree it has been a pleasant hour, *nicht wahr?*

That night I awaited Coenraad in a massive bed. I was perfumed and ready. I was naked under the heavy eiderdown in anticipation of the (delirious) night ahead, my half-closed eyes full of images of his body, his hands, of his mouth over mine. I shifted to my left side to calm myself. I was too warm. As I flung the heavy quilt off me, I was reminded that I helped my mother carry a feather comforter, covered in red cotton, in a wicker trunk on and off trains from Radom to Hamburg, from Ellis Island to Toronto. Thoughts of love evaporated. All I could see was weeping women. Against whom should I direct my protests? Against the French torturer in Algeria who consulted Franz Fanon for treatment for insomnia, the torturer who protested he could not sleep nights because his stubborn victims made his work so difficult? . . . A sense of doom turned the room with its silken walls and fine furniture into a ghetto. Now my eagerness for my lover was for another reason: in his presence terrors vanish.

At midnight he came in through the unlocked door, still in his waiter's outfit, propelling a tea cart. I was hungry. I jumped out of bed, ran forward and whipped off the cover of a silver dish. Inside was a revolver. Under a white damask napkin in a bread basket was his makeup kit. I should have been warned by the presence of his professional paraphernalia: perhaps he was still on duty. Coenraad was silent and undemonstrative, keeping his hands at his sides, as I pressed myself against him to reach behind him and untie his waiter's apron. I often have to help him, because of a severed tendon in his right hand (Athens, 1967) which renders ineffective the use of the principle known as the opposing thumb and forefinger. He compensates with his left hand, but not under all conditions, especially if the knot is tight. I often wonder how he manages when I am not with him. He then took off his shoes with a sigh of relief. He did not remove the rest of his clothes. He sat in the reading chair facing me. He had harsh words that sounded like this:

– When will you learn not to trust everyone!

– I cannot live with suspicion.

– You know the rules; take it or leave it.

– There are no rules for weeping women.

– Just don't speak to strangers.

– *Au fond*, as they say, we are all strangers.

– *Exactement.* All I ask is that you refrain from conversations with wives of condemned Nazis.

– You know who she is!

– It is my duty to know these things.

– But she is old and harmless.

– No one is harmless.

– You're paranoid!

– I'm under orders!

– And does the Agency give you permission to make love to me?

– They don't need to; officially you do not exist.

These last words left me silent and profoundly depressed, especially since they were spoken without the movement of a muscle. His face was a waiter's face; it had the gray pallor of one who spends his life under dim electric lights. He added:

– Moreover, when will you learn to lock your door? You endanger me with your carelessness.

It was just as well I had made no mention of having been followed in my walk along the Elbe.

I have no postcards of Hamburg. I want no reminders of a night spent with our backs turned, and of Coenraad getting dressed just as light appeared at a space between the drapes and then slipping out as if I were not in the room.

I was awake still with memories of Hamburg as disquieting as a nightmare. It was true that officially I did not exist. My passport bore a false name. No one but Coenraad knew my whereabouts. Since I was no longer domiciled I did not appear on voters' lists. I was a stranger in the midst of strangers. Not for me the comfort of being recognized by the company I keep. Yet this solitary life had its advantages: if no one cared about me, I need please no one. Except my lover. I was reminded of the time I asked him why, with an entire world of women, literally, to choose from, why it is me he loves. At that moment I was being held and kissed so that his reply can be recalled in its meaning only. I think he said something that indicated that he, too, is subject to nightmares; that he could not go on unless someone loved him; that he must have something to look forward to and that I was to be trusted.

Did I imagine that there was less vitality out on the streets that next morning? People ambled along as if it were spring; cars meandered as if they were on a country lane. Of course. Friday has become a day of demarcation between the past week's work and the weekend's (anticipated) pleasures. And if I have to be alone this week-end, how will I put in the time? In any other city, in any other part of the world, there are for me new sights and sounds to excite the senses. Yet here in the city I have known all my life I do not know what to do with myself.

This time I avoided the main lobby of the Royal York Hotel and went directly downstairs to the coffee shop, not because of any diffidence, but rather because I felt that the lower one goes in the economic scale the faster the service is. Beside the *Please Wait to be Seated* sign, the same hostess was standing. I noticed the pearls had given way to a gold chain over the black dress. Had she decided that pearls, in her position, were somewhat pretentious?

She headed towards the rear of the dining room, that is to say, once more away from the windows and towards the kitchen, but after a few steps changed direction and led me to the same table as the day before. I wondered whether it was my (now established) resistance, or my black dress and pearls, similar to her professional dress, or perhaps it was the memory of yesterday's journey and detours that led to her capitulation. A small victory, mine, but I told myself it was a beginning.

This morning, except for the waitress and myself, there were only men in the dining room. I pushed aside the menu with its numbered fare and looked about me. This morning I did not feel it necessary to lower my eyes: overnight I had undergone some kind of change: I found I was not uncomfortable in this roomful of men, even though it still suggested a fraternal order, Elks, Eagles, or Orange Lodge. I was able to stare frankly into the face of a man two tables over: I liked his long bony wrists visible over his plate. To my right, a young man was leaning forward, almost bursting out of his jacket, intense with anxiety as he pointed to papers spread out between his coffee cup and the cup of the man opposite, who, being importuned, moved his head and shoulders as far back as his chair permitted. Almost obstructed from view, so that I had to shift to my left to see what went with his thick red hair, was a handsome face with pink cheeks and blue eyes. Even though they returned my gaze, his eyes were remote.

Then I realized I was repeating a habit I had when I was sixteen: I "tried-on" a possible mate the way I speculated about an expensive dress in a shop window: this one, or that one, would "look good on me." This morning, in contrast to my adolescent habit, I found a number of possibilities my skin could accept: this morning I was not being too selective: "fussy" was my father's term. I even considered a serious dark young man in a corner, perhaps in his twenties, who was, possibly, scribbling love poems, a look of inner turmoil on his face — writing love poems calculated to lead his lady to erotic dreams, as Coenraad must have intended when he gave me a book of Sanskrit love poems.

Moths begin their fatal flight
Into the slender flame;
bees, made blind by perfume
wait in the closing bed.

A longing for my lover made me survey the room again. If he were here, I would have had a sign by now — a look, a gesture, a word I could recognize as the memory or the promise of an embrace.

There was nothing on the faces of the men in this room, I thought, that revealed how their night had been spent; nothing lingered in their eyes that hinted that the previous night had, possibly, been an ecstatic one; did any of them have more than one orgasm? had he been welcomed in his ardor? had his partner been indifferent, simply paying her dues? had he had a wild night with his mistress, coming home after midnight with a story that he had to stay in the stables to look after his mare in foal? All the men's faces were intent on the day that was unfolding before them, last night having been scraped away by the morning shave.

Before long the room bustled with the movement of men leaving; sounds of chairs scraping; it was a quarter to nine. The waitresses slowed their steps and cleared tables and pocketed tips before one of them came to my side. She was the same one as yesterday. She poured coffee into my cup and asked, And how are you today. I replied, Very well, thank you. And how is your little girl? The waitress found it necessary to rest the Silex on the table as if it had suddenly become too heavy to hold in midair. What's she done now! Do you know Elsie, are you her teacher or something? I was struck by her pallor. Although I have never seen a dead person up close, not even my mother, I would think a gray skin like hers, with a slight yellow cast to it, would be called deathly. To my mind, it is cause for concern — whose? hers, mine, the Royal York's? — that she looked so ghostly so early in the day. I fear for her. An irresistible vision appears. I see her floating in the space between houses, over the street, not in her blue uniform but in the printed housedress she wears on her days off. I watch her as she falls awkwardly, arms dangling, legs bent, her skirt lifted as if the wind had begun to undress her. In my vision, she never reaches the pavement. I ask the waitress, not in so many words:

– Why don't you want to live to see your little girl grow up?

– What has she been telling you? She makes things up, you know.

– It is against the law to kill yourself. You have no right to end a life that belongs to Elsie.

And the waitress, waiting with pencil over pad, her eyes flat and empty, replies, silently:

– I can't go on any longer. It is too hard; to work, work, work; to live this way, in one room in an attic. And Elsie looks more and more like her father. What if she turns out to be like him? She even talks the way he does, her words run together and I can't make out what she says. It reminds me of his rages. I left him to make a fresh start. My life now is worse than ever. And if a man moves in with me, so that I can have a room with a kitchen, or an apartment even, she tells him lies about me, and tells me lies about him. It doesn't matter who it is; he never stays long, a year or so. What am I to do with her? I cannot go on this way.

– Think, think of the future, think of what Elsie will have to live with the rest of her life if you do away with yourself. For a reason that she will never understand, you will wake her up early some Sunday morning, while the street lamps are still on, at this time of year probably, and you will say to her, Stand right here, and you will open the attic window and jump. You live in a crowded district, so that even at that hour, someone is awake and has seen you fall. The police find their way to the window where Elsie sits still, and snatch her back from the open space. She is safe. At any rate, Elsie is alive. Elsie asks herself then, and forever, what she did wrong that her mother would want to kill herself.

– She will be better off without me. She cries a lot.

– Let me tell you what will happen even though you will be dead and indifferent. As long as she lives, Elsie will recall every detail of that dawn: the pyjamas she wore, pink flannel with blue flowers, putting on her bedroom slippers like you always told her to, not to walk barefoot on the cold floor, although your own feet were bare, following you across the room, not questioning anything, not even your climb out the small window. From that morning on she will not want to look at a pink-streaked dawn again.

– I have pills. I will look as if I'm asleep, that's all.

– And five minutes after your body has been found, your lover will arrive to declare his devotion, with flowers for you and presents for Elsie.

Her lips tremble; she bites them.

– You're trying to make me change my mind. It's too late. I will leave a nice note.

– Oh those notes, red herrings all of them! The imagination knows no bounds before the final act. *I love you. I can't live without you. My life has no meaning. Therefore I will end it. Goodbye cruel world I go to a better one.* And the instructions! At the graveside, as the coffin is being lowered, they are to play a recording of Walter Huston singing *September Song*. At the funeral parlor a continuous showing of the film *Children of Paradise*. She, he, is to be laid out in her, his, wedding garments. And so on. Besides, you can't be certain your note will be found by your lover. I know a failed writer whose hobby is collecting suicide notes — he beats the ambulance to the scene. He intends to publish them as found novels. He will write the setting, description of the dead protagonist, give the text of the note, and the reader will create his own novel. Every reader a writer, he told me, a suicide note is a work of fiction. But Elsie will know the truth: you cannot outwit her with a note.

Her expression changed from despair to one of puzzlement. She wrote something on her pad and left abruptly. When she came back she brought orange juice and hot porridge, which, apparently, I must have ordered. She inquired whether I wanted the eggs the same as yesterday, scrambled. The dark young man at the corner table looked up from his paper. Our eyes met. I reflected, even if he could not care about me, he might, being a poet, like to hear my thoughts on suicide. This wayward notion derived from Coenraad's insistence I forget the past: he wants to know nothing about it: he tells me the moment is all. Coenraad, who, possibly, helps decide the fate of nations; who, possibly, holds untold lives in his hands; who, possibly, is on the side of terror — this man speaks to me of the destiny that arranged for us to meet and fall in love. "I believe in fate," he tells me. Perhaps the young man's stare has nothing to do with me: he may be inviting a felicitous phrase or *le mot juste* and I am in line of his unseeing gaze. Whatever his reason, I recognized my examination of him to be a means of trying to live in the moment: I became again the complete observer, noting how he furrowed his brow and that he tapped a silver ballpoint pen against his teeth. Steadily I ate my Number Four, leaving all the plates clean, and using all the cream provided. I had only to lift a wrist and my bill was brought. Then the waitress joined her young man at his table. I noticed she sat on a corner of the chair, ready to get up and leave quickly if it became necessary. Their heads were bent over the paper from which he appeared to be reading.

Subways, tubes, metros — I am always uneasy in a steel car under the ground, afraid the automatic doors will not open, or afraid that the automatic doors will open in a dark passage too narrow for escape. We sit with fists clenched. I concluded that in a subway, because flight is impossible, we prepare to fight. I was happy to surface and get out at Dundas Street. From the corner I watched a streetcar six blocks away come waddling towards us. It stopped with all its doors open. We embarked in a leisurely manner. The conductor was calm, straightening out transfers against the palm of his hand while answering questions. We pushed gently against one another until seats were found. On a streetcar I feel safe. Every two blocks I have a choice of staying on or leaving. I pull on a cord overhead and the conductor is alerted to my intention. I have but to step down one step at the exit and the doors fly open.

At Parliament Street I got off as if I, too, were in a hurry to get home. Crossing these streets I began to question my choice of Elm Grove. I was in a zone reserved for the poor. The narrow houses were joined in twos or fours and looked as if they were holding each other up at drunken angles. When the sunlight broke through, it was as bleak as the scene it shone upon. I consulted the map. This was a false gesture, as false as the blue plastic hyacinths stuck in the grass beside me — I knew every street in the area, including the one I was seeking; I knew also that "grove" is a misnomer for a mean street with barely a shrub on it.

Occasionally I passed a huge old mansion sprawling back from the street at the end of a large lawn of weeds. I looked up at its windows and found myself playing again a childhood game. By noting whether the glass had been cleaned, the styles and material of curtains, how far down a blind had been drawn, I guessed whether there was inside an old man (lace curtains), the last of a respected hierarchy, who would be found a week after his death; whether there was a pair of elderly sisters (chintz drapes) and their fat, middle-aged nephew, whom all the little girls have been warned against; whether the house had two kitchens (flowered plastic) one upstairs and one down, the upstairs tenancy always short-lived; or, whether its many rooms provided sanctuary for pensioners, deserted women and children, single men of all ages in various stages of sobriety (green blinds only, pulled to the sill) all of whom share the original bathroom on the second floor, which was, after all this time, in remarkably good condition, except for a door which one always had trouble in locking. I felt I should have sought out one of the other Elm streets, in Rosedale perhaps. Even before I got to Elm Grove I knew there was little chance of finding Coenraad in Lower Cabbagetown.

Still, the habit of hoping was strong and I kept turning corners. Number Four was a large house but it had none of the Victorian embellishments of curled wood and moulded plaster. It was plain red brick with plain windows. It looked like a converted warehouse. Three cars were parked on the gravel that had replaced a lawn. At the eastern edge of the property, close to the sidewalk, was the raw stump of a felled tree, its growth rings clear and dark at the outer edge, and dark spots in the pattern toward the center. I checked the journal: *"Look for vascular discoloration in outer sapwood of elm infected with Dutch elm disease."* My hopes rose: if I have deciphered the message correctly, everything points to my having arrived at our rendezvous: the street name with an elm, the house number the same as the number of journal pages, and the large tree trunk clearly has the marks of a diseased elm. As for the one anomaly, the signs of poverty, I recall Coenraad once cautioning me, Take nothing for granted; nothing is predictable.

The house before which I stood was set well back from the street. I looked up at a black door with a brass knob. Facing the black door I got a sudden image of a coffin with brass handles. Inevitably, my mind darted to another conclusion: the journal was sent to me by the Agency as a message that Coenraad is dead. Or worse, that Coenraad has himself sent the journal as a sign that our love is dead. Maybe the very elements of uncertainty and danger that fired our love have proved too much for him. If he found it necessary to reduce risk, I would probably be the first to go. All this while I have been staring at a sign that finally impinges on my mind: *Domino Costume Company. Ring and Enter.*

The hall inside was bright enough but the effect remained funereal, with black carpeting that continued up the stairs and black slabs of doors all about me. How long I stood there, tense and listening, I do not know. Always in situations involving fear and uncertainty I lose my connection with time, not in the sense of "I lost track of time," but in the absence of the feeling of time itself passing, somewhat like being under an anesthetic. In order to put myself back on the track (of time), I knocked hard and loud on the door to my right; and then on the one to my left; and once more on the door down the hall. All the doors were locked. I continued in the same manner on the second floor. Here were five (black) doors off a dim corridor. These doors, too, were locked; and no one here, either, to respond to the beating of my fists.

When I quieted down, I became aware of some sort of activity going on overhead. The sounds were those of footsteps, of more than one person, and of heavy objects being moved. At the thought of going up to the attic, there took hold of me a paralysis that I recognized as a struggle against past misery. If I can bring myself to go up there, I know I will find sanctuary of a kind. An attic is distant in every way from the terrors below. If I can make myself go up there, no one will question my presence. Occupants of these aeries can be likened more to sparrows than to hawks. Their loneliness is the result of a nature that has no claws. Whoever is up there (I cannot imagine him to be Coenraad) will know by the careful sounds I make that I am a sister in timidity.

On the third floor landing I sat on bare wood, with my back against a door. I was not surprised that the steep stairs, the walls and the ceiling, through which rain had obviously leaked, had been considered unworthy of redecoration. Coenraad's advice to savor the moment could not apply in an attic. I was about to take stock of my situation — today being Friday, Coenraad would have to fly to his family; there is only this afternoon left; if I go looking for him on another Elm location I might miss him should he come to the hotel — when the door in front of me burst open. Before me stood a huge figure, resplendent in a medieval costume of many-colored velvets and purple silken hose. He was encrusted in gold and jewels, from the glittering crown on his head to the gold chains and ribboned medals across his chest, to the rings on fingers that were poking and prodding a false beard against his cheeks. His beard secured, the formidable figure advanced. By moving my head a little to the left I could avoid the glare of spotlights in the room behind him, and in this way make out his heavy-browed dark face, set in a fierce expression. He frightened me: he could not possibly be my lover: no matter how Coenraad disguised himself, no matter who he pretended to be, I was not afraid. There is always ease — "that inexpressible comfort" someone called it — between us.

– Glad you could make it. We're ready.

I followed him into a room that was very large despite slanting walls. It was bare except for two straight chairs and three spotlights shining down from a track in the ceiling. Coming towards us was a slender young woman in a courtly gown, the bodice drawn so tight that her breasts were raised high under her chin. Clearly visible under the bright lights was a tattoo on her right breast just under the clavicle. It was a half-blown rose in pink with dark blue stem and leaf. He spoke to her in a deep rich voice, She's here now, let's start. It seemed to me that something was expected of me because they did not "start" right away. I took a chance and extracted my pen and pad, turned some pages (the first page had been written on with *My dear children*) and poised my pen. They appeared to be satisfied. Still they did not "start." He addressed me:

– You've been on the second floor?

– The doors were locked.

– We've stored our sets there. The prop men are very good; you will be pleased with the authenticity of the torture chamber, the armory, a treasury, a garden, and even parts of a castle. A decapitated female is in each room except, of course, in the one containing parts to the parapet, from which she (pointing to the tattoo) threatens to throw herself to escape her fate. He turned towards her and said, Stand here, Issa; you have to watch the conductor. To me he said, At the beginning of the second act, we are in my bedchamber, at the window, overlooking my kingdom, which I have just offered her if she does not disobey me. Issa flung back her long blond hair, humming "mi…mi…mi…" in various pitches, while he continued to address me.

– Actually, her sisters should be here to rescue her. I'm extremely sorry the budget doesn't permit two or more women to join in the lamentations and outcries, the screams and squeals of fear and trepidation. I love a chorus of women's high voices, don't you? Now, then, where are we? Yes. Judith is very curious about my past. Not being satisfied with the shocking truths she has uncovered, she is determined to pry deeper. She has to know everything, at any price. The scene we will do for you is the one wherein Bluebeard and Judith express their love for one another. There is a feeling of hope because of that love. If only Judith will leave well enough alone, if only she will be satisfied with Bluebeard's love for her and all the riches pertaining thereto. (Turning to Issa) You've got the picture: you've just seen the headless body of one of my former wives. You are shaken, but fascinated. More than ever you are resolved to get at the core of my soul; you will not rest until you know everything there is to know about me. The oboe repeats the love theme, then I come in at 46. I plead with you. (Turning to me) This place is too small for full voice, we will have to sing *sotto voce*.

Bluebeard began, singing in a slightly nasal pitch.

B. — You have seen my former loves; they have bled to feed my flowers.

Judith replied in a sweet pure tone:

J. — No more, Bluebeard, no more, no more, no more. I am still here.

B. — Morning, noon and night, they were mine. All my days and nights are thine hereafter.

J. — Bluebeard, Bluebeard, spare me, spare me!

B. — Thou art lovely, surpassing lovely, thou art queen of all my women. (Passionate embrace) Art thou afraid?

J. — Let me have the keys, Bluebeard, give me them, because I love you.

There was a long pause, while they turned pages. I presumed the invisible orchestra was making portentous sounds. Judith continued:

J. — Give me the keys to all the doors. I must enter every doorway.

B. — Tell me why you want to, Judith.

J. — Because I love you. I am here and I am yours. Show me all your hidden secrets; let me enter every doorway.

B. — Thou shalt see, but ask nothing. Look your fill but ask no questions. Judith, love me and ask no questions.

J. — Tell me, tell me, dearest Bluebeard, tell me whom you loved before me?

B. — Kiss me, kiss me, ask me nothing.

J. — Tell me in what way you loved her, was she very fair, did you love her more than you love me, my Bluebeard?

B. — Kiss me, kiss me, ask me nothing.

J. — Let all the doors be opened.

B. — Judith, Judith, I must kiss thee. Come, I'm waiting.

J. — Let all the doors be opened.

Tender kisses and sensual delight were acted out before me less than five feet away.

Ordinarily, opera librettos do not appeal to me: they are for the most part absurd tales of obsessions with love, terror and death; but the poignancy of Bluebeard's dilemma, together with their beautiful voices, moved me to stand up and shout "Bravo!" Bluebeard and Issa bowed to me in a manner so professional that I realized they took me to be a person of artistic sensibilities, perhaps even a music critic. I continued to write in my notebook. The movement of pen on paper seemed to please them, for Bluebeard smiled down at Issa and she smiled up at him. What I wrote was, *I am a person of artistic sensibilities; in order to wear the mantle of the artist one has only to put one's arms through the sleeves.*

As a novice in the art of deception, I was not certain what to do next. If I stayed and explained I was not who they thought I was, they would have felt they had wasted a magnificent effort on me and perhaps would become angry. I said I had to get back in time for my paper's deadline and needed to know their names and so on, at which point Bluebeard went into the room and came back with some glossy fliers colored pink and green. His picture in costume and beard was on one side, looking menacing against the background, which I recognized to be Casa Loma. In the lower right-hand corner was a small photograph of Issa wringing her hands. Bluebeard then impressed upon me the names, dates and prices printed on the other side. I read that the opera *Bluebeard* was by Béla Bartók. I put the writing pad back into my purse, said thank you, and descended the stairs with an air of purpose.

As soon as I was around the corner and out of sight I sat down on the steps of a bungalow. I assumed the house was empty; its windows had been replaced by plywood. I had to consider my situation which had been brought to a crucial point today, Friday. There were twenty-three streets named Elm yet to be checked out. I began to doubt my interpretation of the message. On the other hand, by four o'clock Coenraad might send another message for next week's rendezvous. The best way of spending the next few hours, charged as they would be with anxiety, I decided, was to distract myself with a movie.

The splendour that was Loew's of memory has given way to an efficient system of five small theatres. I chose *The French Connection*. All about me, scattered one or two to a row, waiting for the film to start, were solitary men and solitary women. Am I one of the loners? I wondered, somewhat surprised at the association, yet having to admit that I was in the same position as they, sitting in a dark movie house in the middle of the afternoon because I had no reason to be elsewhere. Or, perhaps, we were all taking a breather, having a respite, declaring a moratorium, from whatever it was we were supposed to get on with. We sat upright, facing straight ahead, purse on her lap, overcoat neatly folded on the empty seat beside him, waiting for the lights to go off. Cheery march music came from two speakers in the corners beside the (curtained) screen; blue, green and red strobe lights chased each other along the two walls. The music ended, the overhead spotlights were turned off, the curtain parted, the screen was white for an instant then images of a film "Coming Soon" covered it.

Fernando Rey is killed in Marseilles, after a long chase along the Old Port by Gene Hackman. He is killed in the Pare du Pharo, in sight of the green slopes where Coenraad and I stretched out in the sun. *Connais-tu le pays?* We knew the country, didn't we, you going back and forth to Marseilles and I riding the tour buses every day, and then you returned to Aries at midnight and in the dark with your arms about me I would describe what I had seen but you were silent about where you had been. You laughed, then remarked how difficult it is for the young when I told you about the graffiti in English on a wall near the University, "Masturbation is the only solution."

Out again on Yonge Street, I made my way against crowds hurrying home. Apparently many have left work early to extend the weekend. Faces advance and then recede. Traffic is heavy; cars have their lights on, making the afternoon seem like nightfall.

Inside the hotel lobby I took in at a glance that the botanists were leaving. Their luggage was strewn about. There were bits of flora and fauna sticking out of paper bags and out of rolled-up newspaper and out of small flowerpots. There was a lineup, but it was at the cashier's desk, a matter I regarded with relief, since my concern was with the receptionist. The clock behind him marked 4:12. He was ready for me: no mail, no message. In my haste, I had forgotten to limp. I didn't care: sympathy would change nothing: Coenraad was not coming.

The weekend had begun and I would be alone again. Alone and with no meeting to look forward to, the anticipation of which would have filled my mind and made the loneliness bearable, what was there for me to do but go up to my room and look at postcards? . . . Sounds rose in my throat that threatened to force themselves out into a cry. In order to gain control I pretended to examine the booklets arranged in three neat piles on the counter. I picked up *Key to Toronto* and *What's Happening*. The third pile was reprints of the article on Dutch elm disease, the four-page copies folded in a manner to reveal on top the (now familiar) picture of a bare elm tree and the word *Victim!* beneath.

– Where did these come from? I asked the clerk.

– They — nodding in the direction of the lineup of botanists — asked to leave them here. Take one, it's free.

– I have one. It was left in my box.

– Yes, now I remember, I put one in every box.

The habit of motion took me away from the desk, as if I had a clear direction, but actually to hide the shock of knowledge that must have been apparent in my face. All my clever guesses had been wrong; there was no message on the plane; the pages of the botany journal had to do with doomed trees — nothing else. I had been entirely mistaken.

In a circle under the brilliant chandelier sat a half-dozen shabby grizzled men as if guardians of the botanists' luggage at their feet. Here they would sit all weekend, having wandered in out of the cold. Throughout the day, they would, one by one, without a word or the flicker of an eye, leave their seat and slip around the marble columns to the cafeteria downstairs and fill up on mashed potatoes. They would sit in their overcoats ready to leave if necessary. They will sit so still they will give the appearance of statues. The house detective will be glad of their company on Saturday and Sunday when this hotel becomes deserted. Crossing the lobby I found myself swerving to the right instead of heading for the elevators. The turn I made led me to the bar, whose entrance was stygian and not at all in accord with the promise held out by the sign overhead, *Bacchus Lounge,* in jiggly letters suggesting dance. To the left of the sign was a painted figure meant, I supposed, to represent the god of wine. It looked as if it had been painted by an amateur, perhaps by one who remembered the paintings in the National Museum of Rome of bacchanalian gods. The satyr's limbs were short, out of proportion to his massive hands and large feet. He had a snub nose, baleful eyes and a mouth turned up in a good-natured leer. On his curly red hair was a crown of vine leaves. He wore a loose garment made of purple grapes. On the other side of the sign was the figure of a young woman, an upraised arm holding a jug of wine, her diaphanous dress revealing curves of breast and hip and thighs. She too was garlanded with vine leaves. I took her to be a Maenad who sang and danced for Bacchus. The figures were crudely painted but evoked, nonetheless, images of Dionysian revels. For some reason it had not been my custom to go to bars; perhaps, vaguely, I would have considered the time spent drinking with other men a form of unfaithfulness to Coenraad. While I hesitated in order to become accustomed to the dark interior, four elderly women filed briskly past me, shaking off drops of water from the plastic hoods they lifted carefully from stiff gray hair. Guilt, or a similar feeling, caused me to turn around. As I did so, the detective quickly lowered his head and pretended to be tying his shoelaces, but I knew that, subliminally, he was observing me go into the bar.

Once inside I was pleased with my decision: the dim faces and the low hum of speech gave off an atmosphere of sanctuary. I kept going, dodging waitresses in long black stockings, until I reached the bar. However, the simple effort of getting on to a bar stool became an awkward rear-end maneuver, as I tried to avoid spreading my legs in an unseemly manner. Our heads were mirrored behind three tiers of bottles, which made us look like the fourth tier, but the mirror was darkened so that our faces were indistinct. The pearls at my throat and the men's white collars and cuffs were reflected best of all. We were not unlike Rembrandt's figures with their stark white ruffs at neck and wrist. Without turning my head, I could hear the woman on my left tell her companion, whose gray hair gleamed in the mirror.

– I will be sixty-five next March. I have given my life to that place and now I'm to be thrown aside like a torn shoe. The young ones are breathing down my neck. It'll take three of them to do my job.

– You should have hung on to one of your four husbands.

– Those guys! Total losses. The only man I ever loved died while I was still a bride. For two years we were honeymooning. I should have died in that car with him. Wasted my life anyway.

My imagination fired by her plight, I looked at her reflection in the mirror. A small-brimmed hat over one eye made her appear tipsy. She disappeared from the mirror as she swirled on her stool and faced me.

– What are you doing here!

– Just having a drink.

– Why here, this isn't the only bar on the street.

– I have some time to spend. I'm waiting for a message.

– So you say. But I know — *she* sent you to spy on us.

– You're confusing me with someone else. My name is Lola Montez and I'm here on a visit.

– You're lying, I don't trust you. Nothing personal, you understand. She's out to get me, I took her precious Percy, and she'll never let up until she gets him back. Beat it, honey, or you'll be sorry.

The bartender was busy with bottles and glasses but he kept an eye on her. She puffed furiously at a cigarette that never left her mouth; the smoke caused the eye under the hat to close. This gave her words a comic turn and I smiled. She stubbed her cigarette. When she took a light from her purse, I assumed it was to start another cigarette. Instead, she thrust the fire in my face. Beat it I said, she said. I slid off the stool and made my way across the room, bumping into people. I took an empty table in the corner, not having the courage to seek the company of others, who, like myself, were alone, even though many looked up from their drinks in a friendly way.

There was laughter and animation all about me. Within an hour the waitress and the bartender and I remained the only ones in the Bacchus Lounge without a drinking companion. I reflected that in a place like this my ability to sit by myself brings me only a request to give the order for another (the third) drink. All the same I looked about me with interest. I would not have objected if someone had sat down beside me. At that precise instant, I saw, framed in the doorway, allowing his eyes to become accustomed to the semi-darkness, the botanist I thought of as "the Mennonite," because of the cut of his beard. I waved to him. He walked towards me without hesitation.

– There you are! You promised to let me read your paper on *Ceratocystis ulmi*.

He was still wearing a name tag pinned to his lapel. *Andrew O'Hara*, and underneath, *Senior Environmentalist*. Somehow O'Hara is not a name I can associate with Mennonites. He ordered a double martini.

– There isn't any paper. I am not a botanist. I am not who you think I am, I said.

– *I'm* not who I think *I* am. Let me explain. When I was fourteen years old, a woman came up to me one day after school. She called me by name, the name, that is, given me by my adopted parents. She said, would you like a hamburger and coffee at Fran's? Sure, I said. At the restaurant I followed her to the very back. She chose a table for two. She faced the wall. There was nothing else for her to look at but me, and that she did steadily. She ordered a double martini for herself. She watched me eat. Now and again she asked how I was getting on in school, hoped

I was studying hard, what would I like to be, an engineer, a doctor? In between she just stared. I had a hot-fudge sundae and she had another double martini. Before we left she asked if I needed anything and insisted I take a five-dollar bill. I was in my second year of high school. For the rest of that year, she was at the foot of the steps waiting for me every Monday. I figured that must be her day off. Each week it was the same: the same table, the same stare and the same questions: well, young man, and how are you getting along?; well, Andy, did you work hard at school this week? And the double martinis and the hamburger and sundae and the fiver. I did not speak of this to my mother, who did not like my staying every week "at a friend's for dinner," since the chores were late getting done that night. Besides, she wouldn't approve of my taking up with a stranger, something I had been warned against, she hinting at unspeakable dangers.

I imagined all sorts of reasons for this lady's concern. Whoever she was, she was the first person who seemed to care about me. Always I came back to the thought that she was my real mother, although there was nothing in our appearance, hers and mine, to connect us. She was short and plump and very dark, with tiny hands and feet. In Victorian fiction she would have been called Eurasian. She had the most amazing smile, perfect white teeth. Many times I wanted to ask her directly, Are you my mother, was I illegitimate, did you give me up for adoption, do you want me back as your son now? I was afraid to ask: either way, yes or no, my distress would have been more than I could handle. The last Monday in May she did not show up. I waited all that day, and the next week, and the next. I never saw her again. I never found out who she was. My mother had no interest in me. At sixteen, she handed me my adoption papers, told me to get out, I was old enough now to look after myself, she said.

– People can be so cruel, I said.

– Please don't cry, he said.

– And your name, whose is it?

– I have always had it; it is mine now. Your name ...?

– I use the name Lola Montez. She was a beautiful, clever and brave woman.

– Why not your own name, the one your parents gave you?

– When I look in the mirror, I see my mother's tragic face.

– There are no mirrors where I live. With me you can be whoever you are.

– Do you mean I'm to go with you?

– No etchings. A roomful of orchids. They are my hobby.

– How can you play around with delicate flowers when the elms are in danger of extinction?

– That pains me too. I've seen men in overalls come and mark the snags with a large X in white paint. I've watched as other men in overalls come and cut the elm down and feed it into a whining insatiable machine, branch by branch. Only the stump is left.

– When I was a child, impoverished mothers and children in summer were given a week in the country in Bolton. It was open farmland; sometimes it became impossibly hot. I remember an afternoon when we sneaked out of our tent at rest hour. We walked along a side road lined with tall, stately elms. We lay in the broad shade of a tree.

– In a few instances, trees have been known to recover completely from an attack because of their ability to seal off the infection under layers of more resistant tissue.

– Have you seen how their leaves in summer yellow and curl and droop?

– Take heart. The Parks Department has planted a more hardy variety called Quebec elms on Elm Avenue.

– Which Elm Avenue?

– In Rosedale. Redundant, perhaps, but it's a start. Do you like music, Viennese waltzes, Hungarian dances? I'll play music for you; you will be at ease.

– Preparation is necessary: I cannot change my hopes all at once.

– Tomorrow is always a proper time. This is where you'll find me (writing on the back of the cardboard coaster), I have no phone.

Solemnly we shook hands. I left.

Once beyond the arch of the lounge, taking leave of Bacchus and his grapes, I had to go back through the lobby, aware of the sharp eyes of the detective, who, it seemed to me, had not moved from his place. I had to go into an empty elevator again, and then along the dimly lit, empty corridors to my room; the key was inserted into the lock; there was the soft *plop* of a lightbulb that failed when I flipped the hall switch. Awaiting me was the packet of postcards on the night table under the lamp. And when I lay back against the pillows later, ready for a night of reverie and dreams, I couldn't find a single card to suit me. Tonight they all looked like what they were: colored pictures of faraway places. Tonight my imagination stubbornly clung to the image of Andrew O'Hara framed in the doorway and the feel of his soft hand.

I gave up the random choice. Instead, I went over my memorabilia, card by card, until I found the one that was certain to elicit such joy that, sometimes when it turned up accidentally, I had to put it at the bottom of the pack lest it keep me awake. It was a photograph of the Drake Hotel in Chicago. That picture pulled me back through a maze of halls, into one of its one thousand and eighteen rooms, to the fourteenth floor, number 1432, the second one to the right of the elevators. This card, recalling the night Coenraad first made his appearance, filled my mind with a clarity of detail that one sees in shock, as after a blinding explosion or during a night of labor. And even when the shock is the result of violent pleasure, then the ordinary properties of wood or plastic or paint or cloth take on strange and mysterious shapes and colors. The senses sharpen as if one's very life were in danger, even in paradise.

That night in Chicago I was in a deep, black and empty sleep, having swallowed three sleeping pills from my hospital hoard. I woke, or rather I was alerted out of sweet oblivion by a sense of something or someone in the room. I could see nothing, but slowly became aware of a presence that moved at the foot of my bed. Suddenly the room was flooded by a blue-white light from the television screen across the room. There was no sound. I sat up and saw a horse and rider galloping towards the horizon. In the somewhat drugged state I was in, I took the rider to be my husband, Zbigniew, and believed he had caught up with me. I was relieved when a close-up revealed him to be John Wayne.

It took courage on my part to shift my glance slightly to the right of the television set, where the intruder sat in an easy chair. He sat across the room, one leg over the other; and one side of his face was illumined by the cold glare of the TV. It came to me that I was not afraid of him, and this in itself frightened me. Except for a broad, rounded forehead, his features were small; and his skin and hair in that light seemed to be without color. I imagined his eyes to be blue. (They turned out to be gray.) He held a finger to his lips, and another was pointing to a connecting door through which he must have come. I nodded that I understood. At that exact moment we had our first intimation of total confidence in the silence between us.

I see him yet, his head to one side, listening. I listened too and heard sounds in the next (his?) room, as if furniture was being moved, then the click of a door, followed by the pneumatic wheeze of the elevator. By how I was wide awake, alert not to danger, but to possible adventure. He slumped in his chair, then rose. I saw he was about to speak, and, most likely, to leave. This time I put a finger to my lips and made room for him on the bed. We continued to watch John Wayne soundlessly fight his way out of an ambush. When the test pattern came on, neither of us moved. I imagined that in this city of gangsters it was not yet safe for this handsome, desirable man to go back to his room. In a whisper I offered sanctuary. Coenraad (it was) began slowly to remove his shoes. Do all men, I wondered, take so long to untie their shoelaces?

In the midst of it all, just as I was concluding that I would know this man's face, this body, from now on, anywhere, with or without clothes, I felt my own body obliterating every thought. I didn't want to leave him for an instant: but my body made the choice: it abandoned him. Coming back, unbelieving, I saw, even in that ghastly TV light, his face still above me, radiant and smiling. Then I turned off the television.

While he slept I listened to the city awakening. The night hum of distant motors gradually came closer. A truck shifted gears in the street below, then rolled away like thunder. A car was heard, then another, and another, until the familiar sounds of traffic filled the air outside. A glint of gray light appeared in the space between the drapes.

While I slept, he slipped away as silently as he had arrived. He left behind him only a hollow in the pillow.

In all this time I have never thought of what would become of me were I never to see Coenraad again. Another kind of daily life will have to begin. Starting anew has always meant for me leaving behind one thing for something better. I leave behind the broken wardrobe for a room with a closet; I reject a seat on an assembly bench for an upholstered chair at a typewriter; I give up two rooms and move to four; I escape a ten-roomed house for a hospital ward — always a trade of some sort. If, for reasons he has hinted at, Coenraad does not meet me again, what will I exchange for my nights with him? Perhaps I will exchange a half-life of waiting for a life I have not tried yet. It was something to think about.

Now think, I told myself, try and remember, did Coenraad ever say in so many or so few words that he wanted to see you again? Did he, after consulting his little black book which he always did in the lull between loving and eating — did he ever say, Darling, my next assignment is London, I wish you could meet me there? Admit it: between the first wild clutch and the last turning away nothing was ever said to indicate that he wanted to see you again. Admit, too, that you learned to time your entreaties so that you extracted promises from him in those exquisite moments before lovemaking. You had discovered that afterwards his lassitude persisted until it became indifference. Then you became frightened. You see that now, don't you, I asked myself: the only thing that keeps you from panic is the knowledge of the next meeting. It is possible, I was forced to admit, he phoned you in Tikal because he could not (would not?) see you again. And for someone's sake, his or yours, he got you back to the city where you live. The rest was born of your desires.

Morning again, after a fretful night. Beside the bed, on the floor, postcards were strewn about. Had they fallen or had they been discarded?

Opening and closing the door again, going along empty corridors and into an empty elevator, pressing the button marked *Lobby*. The lobby was deserted, except for the ubiquitous old men in a row under the brilliant chandelier, sitting as still as sparrows on a wire. I was about to wave to them in greeting, but there is danger in such unthinking reflexes, nothing else. I was afraid that I had finally capitulated to vacuity. I became aware of having approached the reception desk and was now standing before the clerk and that I had done so without conscious will. Certainly I was standing there without any hope. He greeted me by my (false) name. Then he turned around to my box, from which he extracted a small white envelope and held it aloft in the air before me, as one does with a gift to a child. Confusion set in. Have I been mistaken about my mistakes? It was a note and a shiny brass key from Andy. "I am on the third floor. I won't hear the bell. Let yourself in." I could not share the clerk's enthusiasm; I whispered, Thank you.

This morning, anxious to leave the streets which were darkened by towering buildings, I hastened to the corner of Yonge and Front streets, where the structures were low and the roads broad, and where the day that lay ahead of me was bright and cloudless. A crisp wind from the lake blew against my face. Street sounds were different, too. They were sounds that, to me, marked the start of days and nights given over to the pleasures of the city, without the roar of trucks, without the salesmen in a hurry screeching against sudden stops. There were just a couple of buses, and, for the most part, family cars loaded over the passenger limit, rolling slowly, the freshly washed metal glinting in the sun.

I could not claim today to be searching for Coenraad — it was Saturday and he would be home for the weekend — and I walked on, towards Bay Street, enjoying the freshness of the day. The sky was blue, pure and unheeding. Crossing with the light, I felt a weightlessness, or, rather, the end of a heavy weight, as one experiences the first time out of bed after childbirth. I was so light of foot that as I walked I felt a balance between me and the law of gravity. I felt also the disappearance of ghostly consorts. Still, simultaneously with the release, a terror took hold of me at being without encumbrances. I remembered the Latin word for baggage was *impedimenta*. I got a sense of being unimpeded.

When I was forced to come to a stop by a street photographer, a lean young man in a green corduroy suit who stood feet astride in my path, I became angry. He had apparently taken my picture. He offered me the print for a dollar. I uttered a sharp No! He could not have known that he copied a likeness I no longer wanted. He persisted in holding the picture up to me, saying, It's no use to me. Nor to me, I answered. He tore it up before my eyes; tossed the glossy bits into the gutter. Perhaps, it occurred to me, through the "evil eye of the box" the photographer had removed a soul that was weary of wandering. Despite the breeze, the pieces of my soul just lay there. Good, I said to myself. Good riddance.

The coffee shop at the Royal York was lively with laughter and loud talk and the brisk steps of harassed waitresses. Beyond the *Please Wait to be Seated* sign I could see families indulging in breakfasts of pancakes and sausages. The children obviously recognized the privileged nature of the event and poured endless streams of syrup over everything. Finally, a hostess in the shiny black costume known as hostess pyjamas led me to a small table. In my line of vision was a large glass container marked *Vitality* in zigzag lettering to denote the energy of both lightning and of the orange juice within; the liquid cascaded down the sides and over the top of the container in a continuous niagara. I did not see the waitress of the previous days, whom I had come to think of as Elsie's mother. My order for Breakfast #1 was taken by a pleasant woman with wide hips and gray hair. Her "diamond"-framed glasses sparkled. She leaned towards me while she carefully placed the hot coffee at my elbow and said, in a confidential tone, Isn't it lovely to be out on a lovely morning like this?

Except for a dreary room in a deserted hotel, I had nowhere to go. There were still the public places, of course — galleries, movies, museums. Yet, despite their easy accessibility, these harbors did not tempt me today. I didn't want to kill time any more. I dug into my purse and found the paper coaster from the Bacchus bar, Andy's note and key. They were in the zippered compartment, which, until last night, had held only the pictures of my children and of Coenraad. I studied Andy's script; I liked it; the letters were large, all joined; tiny circles over the i's; the t's crossed a third of the way down; the lettering even and straight, not slanted either to left or right. The spaces between the words were generous. The handwriting could be described as optimistic. I memorized the address and replaced the coaster. Before pulling the zipper I studied Coenraad's picture for quite some time.

I tossed some coins on the table with a firm flourish and went towards the exit, where I pushed ahead of a family delayed by the demands of a little girl for gum, but still had to wait my turn. I could not help but compare the weak bleeps of the electronic machine with the huge brass cash register at which my stepmother used to sit as if chained. No one, not even my father, was allowed near her temple of Mammon. It's not for me, I swear, my father swore, it's for Shirley; she needs shoes. I'll give you back when I go back to work. But she was adamant: Shoes she'll get if she helps in the store.

I helped in the store; my father got a job; but neither he nor I were ever allowed near the cash register.

A revolving door at the side entrance to the Royal York took me out to a lane. The driver of the first of a long line of taxis looked directly at me; the temptation was strong to take a cab to Andy's. We eyed one another, until he was forced to turn away because of my (obvious) decision not to hire him. I looked towards my left, considering subways, shows, stores. I went, instead, to the right on Front Street. It stretched to the west endlessly, empty, deserted. At York Street I was exposed to yet another temptation: the airport bus was awaiting passengers, its luggage hold wide open. I looked straight ahead, crossed the road, and kept going. I was not in any hurry, having decided to take a stroll in the sunshine and, possibly, think of what I will do without Coenraad. It was easy to concentrate, since there was not another person in sight.

After a while I felt I was walking in forbidden territory; I had a sense of danger that comes when one asks why is there no one here but me? The yellow cruiser moving slowly at the curb beside me stopped. A young, clean-cut policemen jumped out in front of me and startled me with his look of hatred, a look of viciousness that somehow did not belong with his pink-cheeked youth. I think he said, What are you doing here, can't you see that all the buildings are being torn down, haven't you any more sense than to expose yourself to unknown hazards, don't you realize that danger lurks in parking lots, have you any identification? I was, indeed, the only person, except for my inquisitor, on the street. Ominous sounds came from giant plastic sheets flapping in the wind, sheets that draped the fronts of old red brick buildings, sheets meant either to protect the pedestrian from loose bricks or to hide the shame of vandalism that precedes reconstruction. I handed over my wallet with driver's license, social security and credit cards, all visible through plastic windows. The policeman began to copy numbers into a little black book. When he came to the credit cards, of which I have nine, his expressions went from belligerence to uncertainty to apology. Sorry, ma'am, but we have our orders you understand we can't be too careful, so many creeps here for the weekend from Buffalo and Detroit. He tore out and crumpled the page he'd been writing on. Just the same, ma'am, for your own sake I suggest you leave this area.

Around the corner, on John Street, I was on home ground. A little further down, at Wellington, I could see the blackened windows of the Admiral Building, where, on the fourth floor, my dexterity in pushing wicks and stuffing cotton into cigarette lighters had earned praise from the foreman. Continuing north here on Adelaide Street, between John and Simcoe, I looked up at a warehouse, where I once typed two thousand envelopes a day for a mail-order company. When I came to Queen Street, I automatically turned to my right and found, a couple of doors from the corner, that Wexler's Restaurant was still in business, although today, Saturday, they were closed, since they are open only when factories are open. The same dusty glass comport was in the window, but the years had leached all the color from the wax oranges, apples, lemons and bananas. The false fruit now was a shade of dirty ivory. In the window, nearest the entrance, and easily reached into by the cashier, were four large paper bags full of styrofoam cups ready, I presumed, for Monday morning's take-out. I mused on the nature of social democracy in those days. No matter what my job was I was free to sit anywhere, even beside the owner of a dress company or his accountant. The only difference between us was the type of lunch: either a thick Kaiser roll with cheese; or gefilte fish, chicken soup, roast chicken, strudel, prunes and tea with lemon. If you could afford it, every day was Sabbath.

Now, ahead of me, a block away, were the four corners of Queen and McCaul streets; I could see the traffic lights, which had not been necessary in my time. Continuing south on McCaul Street, I found the same houses I had known; on most of them the bricks had been repainted. Absent were the black cardboard signs in the front windows that had offered, in red letters, *Room To Let* or *Flat To Let*. And when I came to Dundas, I could see the Art Gallery and thought of going in since Saturday afternoon was almost as good a time as Sunday, but, for the first time, I was not drawn to shoulder my way through the revolving doors. For, at this point, people began to appear on the street and I wanted to share the sun with them. There were mothers and children, families of various relationships; students, couples. Nobody was alone.

All were absorbed in one another in a way that reminded me of walks with Coenraad. In his company, on this street, I would tell him stories about my early life. On the other hand, I might be content just to be at his side; I might say nothing at all: he is quickly bored.

The number on McCaul Street I was looking for was outlined in black wrought iron on a new door beside an old grocery store. The building itself was in the shape of a square box divided in half horizontally, its bricks gleaming with fresh vermilion paint. The store's two windows, at the sidewalk's edge, had *Coca-Cola* logos across their tops, and, on the inner side of the left window, *Cigarettes,* and similarly on the right, *Groceries.* I was on the corner of the western limit of Elm Street; across the road began D'Arcy Street. Finding myself on this corner was a coincidence, I told myself, that augured well for the future and not, as I feared in a momentary panic, of a fateful return to the past.

Andy's key slipped easily into the lock and the door yielded to a light push. And, for once, the flights of steep stairs beckoned: they were brightly lit and clean, with rubber treads all the way to a door at the top. I walked up keeping time to a beat pounding somewhere in a deep bass, as if from a jukebox. The door was ajar. Inside, I found myself in a blaze of daylight. Overhead was a skylight that roofed the whole room and revealed the same azure sky.

He must have sensed my presence: he could not have heard me come in with that music beating away. It came from a Wurlitzer just inside the door, to my right. Andy hurried down the long length of the narrow room and shouted, I won it in a raffle. It was the classic of jukeboxes — classic in the sense that it restored an art of the past. The entire machine glowed in an aura of rose. At the top, a massive piece of chrome in Art Deco design was surrounded by neon tubes that gave off lights in yellow and blue and red. The buttons burned red. The speaker was partially obscured by more Art Deco in black celluloid. And down the sides were tubes with streams of pink and green light that flowed steadily. Behind the glass, where three-minute jive records took our dimes, there now was a conventional turntable spinning out a long-playing record — Brahms, I think it was.

On my side of the room, beside the Wurlitzer, were pegs on the wall holding a knapsack, binoculars and a green jacket with many pockets. An army cot was covered with a red Moroccan blanket. Partially hidden under the cot was a pair of dirty hiking boots, the brown leather discolored, gray mud dried around the soles. At the end was a table with a kettle and bottle of wine on it. Across the front of the room were a microscope and shelves of books. The entire length of the wall opposite, under eaves of glass, was taken up by orchids. Orchids in pots plain and adorned, on innumerable surfaces and hanging from beams. Orchids, white and mauve, yellow and violet, green and purple, clear-colored or spotted. Orchids, from whose centres extruded soft lips surrounding stamen. I found myself caught, fascinated, by their erotic shapes. In this room, Andy's red hair and bright blue eyes did not appear so intense; he was part of the color. The quickening shift of the sun suddenly hit the bottle of wine, causing it to gleam like a ruby. I knew that were I to come here again I would not wear black. Andy's excitement at my arrival didn't strike me as such at the time, in the midst of music, the exotic flowers, the geometry of light and shadow, and color everywhere. Only later, while sipping wine, after the sunlight had gone and the Wurlitzer was stilled, did I realize how definite his welcome had been.

Hey! he had said, his mouth close to my ear (because of the volume of music?). Good. Perfect.

But now the sun was hitting the glass directly. I was forced to turn my face away from the dazzling light towards Andy at my side. We were sitting on the cot; there were no chairs.

– I was in the hotel, I explained, waiting for someone. He didn't show.

– Please, you mustn't — it doesn't matter . . .

I wanted to tell him about Coenraad, but some sensibility, perhaps, even, an instinct, made me resist the lure of confession. While I struggled with myself, Andy filled the silence. And as he spoke, I thought, he is no better at idle talk than I am.

– One of Nature's wonders, he was saying, is imitation. Did you know that the blossoms of the *Ophrys insectifera* orchid have evolved to resemble the female wasp so closely in scent, shape, color, even to the furriness of the labellum, that the male wasp enters and attempts sex . . . ? The purpose of this deception, of course, is pollination.

– Do you think I have been deceived?

– No, no. I'm not making an invidious judgement. What I'm trying to say is that we do things out of some mysterious necessity. Then he smiled. Nuance is everything, he added.

Concentration was getting difficult. I remarked on the heavy perfume in the room.

– It's been discovered, Andy continued, that there are at least fifty compounds in the fragrance of an orchid that can be detected by the male wasp as far away as ten miles. What happens next is called pseudo-copulation.

It was a word, I felt, that would some day spark a misunderstanding between us.

Was it his idea of foreplay? I couldn't be sure. He proceeded to show me, scientifically, what happens to the wasp when he enters the brownringed, purple centre of the *Ophrys speculum*. I noticed that Andy's mouth turned up at the corners as in the pictures of satyrs. But unlike their baleful leer, Andy's look was quick and piercing, more Dionysian, I thought.

– The strong odor attracts and intoxicates the wasp. He goes in headfirst. The drunken insect loses his footing; a trapdoor opens; he falls down an oily chute and is trapped in a fluid secreted by the orchid. In the morning, when he comes to, he regains his hold on the florets because they have dried up overnight, and the bee is then able to crawl out a narrow hole. He flies off, taking the pollen with him to the next orchid.

Whether sex or science, the images were funny and I smiled with him. Andy began to bustle happily: more wine? relax, do you like Hungarian dances? I think I must have gypsy blood in me, he said. Still in my thoughts, I drank wine and tried to comprehend the contradictions inherent in the pseudo-real. Phrases like *reality of appearance* and *the illusion of reality* were going through my head: but the music kept distracting me. Music, it is said, is the perfect art. It, too, is an abstraction, at the very least, of vibrations, of wavelengths, of such and such frequencies, of so many overtones, of semitones and quarter tones; yet none of those components, as with fragrance for the wasp, accounted for the rising tension I felt as I listened to Liszt's Hungarian Rhapsodies.

In the course of time, when we make love, Andy takes as his own the rhythms of Liszt's dance. He incorporates into his movements long slow phrases of the right hand, while the left hand sustains a persistent beat, then both hands run up and down the keyboard. The dancers, prepared, take formal steps opposite one another, the movements casual, steady and serious; they move as if saying take your time, we have all night; they get to know each other, sense one another's intentions. A little anxiety is heard in the arpeggios. Can you see the stars above? Andy asks; They're yours. He holds on to me, the music continues a little faster now as we roll over and he lies beneath me, he now looking up at the stars. The dancers tire, the music slows; we wait for it all to begin again, slowly, the music is sad, life is sad, the plight of all lovers is sad, but here we are, in the dance, the music urges us on, faster, faster, yet there is no hurry, we can dance our lives away. In the midst of it all, Andy hums snatches of melody. Now there are variations on themes, the dancers speed up and slow down, halt momentarily, the rhythms alternate, slow, fast, slow, fast; stop; and getting ready for the finale, the music races, chords, trills, arpeggios, the dancers whirl, faster and faster, until, in a joyous crescendo, in time with the crashing chords, they stamp their right heels and shout Ha!

One day, too, after lovemaking, I say, Music is not the only perfect art.

A second bottle of wine had been opened and poured cere-moniously from on high; we watched the red liquid flash in the light. We drank out of pottery mugs. I wasn't certain why I was there, but I was happy, deciding that scales are well-tempered and that nature is teeming. All the same, I sat on the edge of the cot, my feet flat on the floor. Andy suddenly busied himself with slides and microscopes, making notes. He had a way of abruptly look-ing up from his work and staring at me until I met his eyes, and I, unbelieving, wanted to ask, who, me? Even as I was wondering whether to stay or go — the sky had faded into gray with faint streaks of pink in the west — Andy shut the notebook and covered the microscope. He was at my side, murmuring pleasant adjec-tives, some of which had never been addressed to me before.

– Well, he asked, what are you thinking? Will you stay?

– I'd like to, I'm very tired, but there's one more walk I must take before I can decide.

I stood up, keeping my eyes on the orchids, and noting that their colors remained potent in the darkening room. I imagined wasps entering their centres.

– Are you worried about making a mistake? Andy asked.

– No. I've read that a principle in biology is that discovery often depends on something going wrong. Don't misunderstand me: I mean only that I'm not afraid of taking you seriously.

– It's going to be a clear night. Don't go. I'll give you the moon and the stars . . .

A final doubt, unspoken: *when I come back, will I be able to withstand the light?*

If I had not left when I did, much of what I subsequently learned would have remained hidden from me. I continued to take walks and to go in and out of public buildings, but, Janus-like, began to look in two directions — where I'd been and where I was going. The important thing was that behind me now was a door I knew I could open with my own key anytime I wanted to and be welcomed. Andy had been explicit about that. A question had arisen in my mind.

– Interfere . . . your work?

– These . . . told you . . . hobby. I work in an office . . . nine to five. Trips . . . would you like . . . with me . . . in the country . . . Sundays . . . in the woods.

– Agreed . . . if you . . . city walks . . . with me.

I could not help but compare this exchange with an incident in Stockholm. The alarm had rung; Coenraad shut it off; he turned to me. It was not the only time he had ignored the clock in order to make love once more; but that particular morning he fell asleep again and was late for his appointment at the American Embassy. I held out the cufflinks, I placed his overcoat, gloves and hat near the door (it was winter), and as he hurried to dress, Coenraad said, Lucky for me I didn't know you years ago. And I, weak-kneed and seated, replied, Oh, but I wish we had! My life would have been fulfilled! Exactly, he replied, *you* would have been fulfilled, but I would never have amounted to anything.

Outside, on Elm Street, a few yards from Andy's door, a young woman rushed past, pulling a chattering child. The mother was not paying attention, her head strained forward, intent, I imagined, on getting to her own door and preparing supper. Possibly the child was telling her mother that she had been tied down on a cot and that she wouldn't stop screaming, No one could make me stop screaming. Her interest finally caught, the mother looked down on her daughter; but then, perhaps, felt her own helplessness and said, Serves you right; that will teach you; now will you be good?

Near Chestnut Street a half-dozen children played. They ran and shouted, which was just as well, for they were not dressed for the cold. These children have no equipment for games other than thin arms and legs and calculating eyes. It was just after five o'clock, at twilight, that time of day Nerval called *l'heure fatale*; that time of day when the birds are in flocks, and, in the city, are to be seen in the sky between the towers of bank buildings; it was that time of day when the last glow of the sun illumines the bricks and returns them to the fire; that time of day just before the evening meal when the streets empty mysteriously and the grumbling city becomes peaceful; that time of day when lamps are lit in houses.

And then, in that last light, I was buffeted by wave upon wave of sorrow. Maximilian once told me that it was a syndrome called, in German, *weltschmerz*; literally, world pain; the pain of being in the world. It — all my struggle, all my efforts — it had all been to no avail. Just as suddenly, without thought on my part, by itself, came pity — pity for myself, my husband, my children; a pity that encompassed everyone I had ever known, even that landlady with red hair and, strangest of all, Coenraad. I was emptied of all thought: pity filled me completely. Inexplicably, out of nowhere, a minute later, I recall the exact instant, when the sodium vapor lights came on and the street got as bright as day, and I came to Yonge Street and saw the four corners of Yonge and Dundas, saw the bookstore, the clothing store, the Brown Derby, the bank beside me, crowds crossing or waiting to cross, people descending into the subway, a minute later, for no reason at all, I was exultant. It was a joy that comes to children and is without cause. I threw back my head and straightened up and broke into a run. The feeling was akin to triumph.

At the King Edward Hotel I went through the revolving doors with such force that two people behind me had to stand back and wait for the revolutions to slow down. After I had opened the door to my room I made no effort to prevent the resounding slam of the door as I let it swing shut on its own weight. Inside, I stood, two hands on one hip, staring at my pack of postcards. The maid must have picked them up. I thought of the endless hours of the night ahead. Then an anger seized me, perhaps an anger with myself for a failure of courage. I took hold of the cards and wrapped them in the hotel's laundry bag, folded the plastic over and over, then secured the package with the knotted elastic band. The prospect of being without proof of having loved and having been loved caused my hands to shake. I carried the package to the corner of Yonge and King and found a blue enamelled trash can marked in yellow letters *Keep Toronto Clean* and, underneath, *Pitch In.* The postcards were pitched in. It was an act that took its toll: I dropped with them. My stomach lurched; I was nauseated.

What was really odd the next morning was that I was dressed before daylight. Perhaps I had not undressed. I waited for what may have been a long time for dawn, standing to one side of the wired window so that I could see a part of the sky. For the first time since my mother's death I faced the sunrise. It came up again as if nothing had happened. There was a glow of gold, a few longitudinal clouds outlined in rose. Inside the hotel and out in the streets there was an absence of noise, heard as a hum. It was the sound of Sunday. I thought vaguely of Coenraad. He will be getting ready to go to the Episcopalian church with his family. They will enter the church, his wife flanked by two sons, going in first, followed by Coenraad with his daughter at his side. Once through the doors, the images become clouded and dissolve altogether. I have never been inside an Episcopalian church. It would seem that without the background of a postcard, the beloved figure vanishes.

Today, the emptiness and the silence in the hotel did not oppress me. Today, the old men in the lobby, as if sculptured on the edge of their seats, made me feel at home. I appreciated the set of their faces: the catlike quality combining alertness with utter indifference. I waved to them. The house detective sat in their midst: I felt he has been defeated by their independence. I waved to him, too. He did not meet my (independent) look.

Nor did I mind the poorly-lit cafeteria, with its Formica tables and flimsy chairs and puce walls. All I felt was hunger. I wanted to serve all that bacon and all those scrambled eggs to those about me, alone at tables, plowing through platefuls of toast or porridge or fried potatoes only. The cashier asked, How are *you* today? without taking her eyes off my tray while she calculated its worth. She was dressed as if for a party: gold hoop earrings, every portion of her handsome face rouged, shadowed, pencilled. She wore a red flowered dress, cut low in front, a corsage of artificial gardenias pinned to her left breast. I told her I was very well and very happy and hoped she was too. She looked up, startled. I asked her what was the weather like when she came to work and did she mind coming so early Sunday morning. She held my change in her hand, in midair, over mine, while my breakfast got cold, telling me that she would rather be here than alone in her apartment; she spoke of her four grown children, none of whom cares what happens to her; said she would rather be here meeting people than alone in her apartment all weekend. The weather, I repeated, what kind of a day is it? Sunny. Crisp. Cold for this time of year. Snow has been predicted.

Emerging from the hotel, finding myself alone on King Street, I couldn't get my bearings. The usually bustling street was empty, as after some disaster. I had to remind myself that the agents and typists and bankers and clerks and salesmen and investors who crowd these streets would be back tomorrow. The peculiar silence was broken by a peal of bells coming from the spired old church I could see from where I was hesitating on the sidewalk. In the past I avoided taking solitary walks on Sunday. It is a day for lovers. But it is not a day for those whose love is illicit. It is a family day. But it is not a day for families who are unhappy. Now, forced out into the open, as it were, I found myself strolling up Yonge Street. In short order, between King and Adelaide, I encountered, four times, well-dressed (family?) men walking alone. I paused at Simpson's and stood beside a man who was looking at the window displays. He was of medium height, hatted, gloved, tailored overcoat, gray suit, shiny brown shoes — so perfect a costume that he triggered in me a reflexive hope, which I erased at once. Coenraad at this very moment was still sitting in church. I moved on quickly.

As soon as I was able to stop looking at men who reminded me of my lover, I began to notice that there were others like myself, as one with crutches is aware of those similarly crippled. I passed an old woman in a tweedless tweed coat and galoshes with metal buckles; I passed a Chinese boy in a quilted black silk jacket; I passed a curly-haired teenager who, despite the cold, revealed nipples under a sheer blouse; I passed a man who must have just come off the boat, as we used to say, wearing an overcoat with a caracul fur collar and yellow shoes and swinging a brown cane. There were more. We solitaries came towards one another, passed; others came up from behind and passed me; at times we walked side by side for a few paces. Soon I got a sense of a common activity: I thought, I would like nothing better than to link my arm through yours and we would walk along together. Acts of fellowship, I reflected sadly, take place only during bombings and public hangings. Under normal conditions strangers must avoid the other's strangeness.

At Queen Street young people swarmed on the sidewalks. They were of all colors, in pairs and in groups; their many languages reached me as the buzz of bees. They were in a holiday mood, but tense, as if Sunday was going to end very soon and they had to get everything they could out of the holiday. They laughed and pushed and eyed each other in a kind of courtship dance, seemingly indifferent, but alert to the main chance. They took possession of the sidewalk: sometimes I had to step off the curb for them. They infused the street with an air of adventure, of the sort I experienced once before in the streets of Marseilles. No sunny slopes here though, such as the ones in the Parc du Pharo, where Coenraad and I lay in the sun. Afterwards we walked beside the ocean in the Old Port and you said I had to leave Marseilles because the city was dangerous. I said I was not afraid.

And you said that *you* were. You insisted that I take the train to Arles, bribing me with an orange and a piece of cake bought on the steps leading to the St. Charles railway station. In Arles you came to my room at midnight every night and I told you about my daily pilgrimages when I retraced the steps of Vincent van Gogh, but you said nothing of where you had been or what you had done.

I have heard it said that Toronto has become a dangerous city; that people are afraid to be out in the streets at night. I ruminated that I will find cities within cities in Toronto. I will choose. I realized that right now I have no idea, for instance, where these young people come from, where they live, where they work: do they work in factories or abattoirs or stand all day in Becker's or in hospital kitchens, places I have forgotten about? I wished I were not outside their lives. I hung about with them. With them I window-shopped and noticed clothing to be worn either by men or women — shirts, jackets, boots, jeans with flies in front. With them I examined the frenzied figures on posters outside the movie houses, observing that triple bills offered horror and sex and disaster in bizarre combinations. With them I was intrigued by the hundreds of bits of artistry from India or Hong Kong in little shops. With them, too, I stood near an open doorway, the door frame outlined in lights that blinked like myriad flirting eyes. We could see nothing in the darkened interior. Then we turned to gape at photographs under glass mounted on the walls outside of big-breasted naked girls, who had assumed provocative poses, yet managed somehow to hide their pubic triangles. I watched two young men laugh and jostle one another towards the stygian doorway: it looked as if they were gathering sufficient nerve to go inside.

Just by crossing the road at College Street I got the impression that I had moved from excitement to respectability. It was as if the frontier began at the Y.M.C.A., whose sign, a large red triangle, was visible just a little west of where I now was. North of College was territory established by the bourgeoisie (my father's favorite term of contempt). Everyone who passed me was patently on his way to some planned destination, moving with arms swinging.

On approaching Bloor Street, I came upon a long lineup for the film at the New Yorker Cinema. I have seen *Children of Paradise* nine times. It is the only movie I will line up for. But now I must first queue up to buy a ticket, then go to the end of the line. We moved slowly, politely keeping our places, out of the sunlight into the bright lights of the lobby. There was a mass diversion to the candy counter, which gave me an opportunity to select a seat inside in the exact centre of the theater. Then, for the tenth time, I savoured the happiness of Baptiste and Garance; for the tenth time I suffered the lovers' despair; for the tenth time I heard Baptiste tell Garance, *When I was unhappy I slept. I dreamed . . . but people don't like it if you dream. So they knock you about to "wake you up a bit," as they say. Luckily, my sleep was tough, tougher than their blows, and I escaped them by dreaming . . . I dreamed . . . I hoped . . . I waited . . .* My own grief was in such harmony with the plight of the lovers parted by a cruel fate that I felt I had made their story mine. To the stealthy dipping of fingers into popcorn boxes and to the silent sipping through straws all around me, I added quiet tears.

When I came out, the sky beyond the Park Plaza Hotel was in bands of orange and pink. Little crowds waited at the four corners of Yonge and Bloor for the lights to change many times before deciding to cross the street. Some did not cross at all but turned about and went back in the direction they had come from. Is this typical of Sunday behavior? I wondered. I stood in the doorway of Grand & Toy, beside the subway entrance, resisting the magnet of habit, which, in this instance, was to go down the stairs, take the train to Eglinton, a bus to Lawrence, then walk five blocks to my house. The sun set, the streetlights went on, but still I stood there, in the dark doorway, unable to take the next step. What was I waiting for? The question evoked Coenraad once more, and brought to mind that time (I had asked for an anniversary celebration in Chicago) when he had sat out my tears and pleas and, sure of himself, had said,

– That's it. That is all. That is everything. Take it or leave it.

I had refrained from the rejoinder that, to me, "taking it" was as routine as brushing my teeth.

His ghost persisted, Take it or leave it.

Recalling that even in spirit I was dealing with an expert in equivocation, I replied,

– I will give you my answer later this evening. I went down into the subway, pleased.

When I came to Cheltenham Avenue, my street with its centre-hailed family homes, three-storied, lawns and hedges and brightly lit entrances, I strode to my own house halfway down the block and went up the short walk to broad stone stairs, noting the numerous cracks and the loose wrought-iron railing, the cement footings having crumbled. I thought, the entrance will not withstand another winter.

The front door was locked. My hands, groping inside my purse for the familiar feel of the leather case with its five keys (two car, one back door, one front door and bank deposit box), came up empty. At the bottom of the purse were my hotel key on its oversize hardboard tag and Andy's key. I could not remember what I had done with my house keys. Had they been taken from me? There loomed the possibility that I would not be able to get into my own house: it took control not to beat upon the door with my fists. At the same time, paradoxically, I was not sure I wanted to go in.

On this side of the door was a city of streets, subways, taxis, trains and planes. On the other side, inside my house, was an ineluctable sequence of worn words and stale acts. Even so, the choice to stay out or go back inside should be mine to make. I did what the children used to do if no one was home: I went through the gate to the garden and upon the cedar deck; I tried the glass doors opening out from the family room. They were unlocked. I remained on the deck in the dark, however, in order to watch Zbigniew as he slept in his easy chair. The Andersons' dog next door began to bark, but someone put a stop to its alarm.

Under the light of a reading lamp Zbigniew's face in repose is the face of an aristocrat whose ancestors are in the history books of Poland. I have been shown their pictures. They are, like their displaced descendant, men with blond hair, square faces and small nostrils. Behind Zbigniew's large lids are blue eyes, imperious in their gaze, which, now that I think of it, never change their color or expression. Relaxed, his mouth is full and curved; yet I remember it as a mouth with lips that barely open to speak. Awake or asleep I know he dreams of riding his mare across his (no longer his) fields, hunched over the shining back, straining towards a curve in the sky, which he reaches quickly, but he does not stop, because even in that short time the sky has straightened and he sees another curve towards which he must, he absolutely must, with every ounce of his strength, his and his horse's, reach. I see him astride his horse in his grandfather's Cossack costume, his knees dug into the mare's flanks, his bare head against the wind, his coattails flying. And should some barrier suddenly loom up between him and that distant ellipse, he and his mount, the two now transformed into a centaur, will transcend the obstacle in a perfect arc. Such were the pictures evoked for me by my husband in the flowery speech of his youth, which, even in translation, I once found poetic.

That Polish horse-and-rider were no match for the German tanks.

Zbigniew took flight.

In England he put on a blue-gray R.A.F. uniform.

Zbigniew flew like the Polish eagle that was sewn on the left breast of his jacket and on the front of his cap, above the visor. He darted across the skies like the bolts of lightning which were the insignia of the Polish squadron.

My husband is in his old Air Force jacket and cap, and as I continue to observe him through the plate glass, I cannot help but admire how well the jacket still fits him: the three brass buttons are done up; and how well the gray-blue shades become him now that there are touches of gray hair at the temples. As inevitably as the day itself recurs, on Sundays Zbigniew comes home at 4:30 from the stables, showers, puts on a clean white shirt and a dark blue tie and his old uniform jacket and cap, retires to the family room which will be exclusively his for the next four-and-half hours, it having been pointed out to us that the children and I have the use of the room all week long; then he goes through the stack of the week's newspapers, starting with last Monday's on top, speed-reading until he works down to the Sunday paper of that day, which he peruses, usually after dinner, until 9:30, at which time we go up to our bedroom. There he takes off his jacket and cap, crosses himself in memory of the others, similarly uniformed but dead, for he is the sole survivor of his squadron.

But now he lets fall on the floor to his left the paper he has just finished reading and reaches for the next one from the pile on his right. I watch him unfold the newspaper page by page. He sits erect. His hands are strong but soft as velvet. An odd memory of those hands: I used to lie on my belly and he would stroke my back from my head to my heels. Then in my mind at the same time he began to stroke the back of his chestnut mare, with the palms of both hands, from mane to tail, over and over, slowly, lingering briefly at the tail before beginning again with the same rhythm at her neck. Silently, he would continue to stroke me, slowly, beginning at the back of my head, lingering briefly with his fingers between my legs. The image persisted. Then I would see his hand caress the mare's nose, his face close to hers, uttering sharp cries of *Moja kobylko, moja kochana kobylko!* My beloved horse!

Suddenly the paper in his hand is thrust down onto his lap. Something has caused Zbigniew to draw in a sharp breath, open his mouth wide in what must be a shout. A woman comes hurrying in, wiping her hands on a towel. The woman's back is to me; and since Zbigniew is absorbed in what he is reading to her, neither of them sees me pull aside one of the glass doors.

That is me he is reading about.

... and she took a taxi to Emergency, wearing a raincoat over her nightgown, her hair uncombed, in her son's slippers, clutching a large black purse. At the hospital she could only make low moans in reply to routine questions. All the tests, blood and neurological, gynecological, X-rays in three dimensions, a brain scan, revealed no pathological cause for her distress. She claimed to have neither husband, children or other family; nor did she have a family physician. A social worker by examining the contents of her purse established that she had a good city address. A telephone call to that address established that she has a husband and two children and a father. Moreover, in the immediate vicinity there is a private medical clinic, where, it was ascertained, there are records of her, as well as the family. Accompanied by one of the hospital's volunteers (name withheld on request) Mrs. Kaszenbowski was returned to her home, where, she kept insisting, she no longer lives ...

There is a moment, as after the eulogy at a funeral, when the words are allowed their full impact, considered, then weighed against the facts. Zbigniew let fall the paper, his hands limp at his sides. He and the woman were silent. Zbigniew fell back against the chair, the movement causing his cap to tilt forward so that his eyes were covered by the leather peak, giving him the air of a rake, a look so foreign to his nature that I had to stifle my laughter. The woman stood before him stock-still, with her head bowed. In her place I would have done the same: she was probably hiding a smile. Then he said,

– I saw no reason for a private room. The practice of medicine does not alter with the number of beds. She received the same care and the same treatment in the public ward.

There was for me a certain satisfaction that the newspaper report had had some impact on him. Moreover, when they left the room, the woman went ahead and Zbigniew followed with a step that resembled a shuffle. The evidence of his discomfiture gave me the courage to leave the garden and go around to the front door and ring the bell. I was moved also by a desire to see the faces of my two children. This feeling was immediately followed by a resentment that the woman would be summoning *my* children; in turn followed by the thought that I could, legally, oust her if I wanted.

She opened the door.

– Oh, it's you! I've been expecting you.

She welcomed me, I felt, by the way she held the door open wide, and swung her free arm in a manner that ushered me inside. Perhaps she had recognized me from the family snapshots in an album at the bottom of the buffet drawer, under the tablecloths. I stepped into the hall.

– I knew you'd turn up sooner or later, she said affably. She seemed completely at ease in my house, as if she had always been there; whereas I experienced the kind of embarrassment one is made to feel in entering a museum near closing time. She was taller than I and much thinner, so that my black jersey dress was held up by bony shoulders and pulled together at the waist by a man's brown leather belt.

— My name in Francesca, she said. I was born in 1922 in Toronto on Grace Street, just above Dundas, in an attic room in a house owned by people named Tannenbaum. My mother refused to have another child, said she'd kill herself first, unless she could go to a hospital for her confinement. When I was eight she did kill herself, much to my father's bewilderment, since, as far as he knew, he had never harmed her in any way. Somehow he managed to keep the police out of the situation — he was a clever man — lest the Children's Aid take me from him. I was forbidden to speak of my mother's death to anyone. I forged her name on notes to school. We moved after that to Clinton Street, above College, to a better house, owned by a couple named McGregor, again to the third floor. Despite the heat in summer and the cold in winter, my father preferred the cramped, dark enclosure of an attic room, for his studies, he said. He was removed from the encroachments of sordid bourgeois life, he felt. In his youth he had been an anarchist in Milan. He was arrested many times. Once he went on a hunger strike and came down with typhoid fever. His health was destroyed. I used to prepare the same meals for him every day; he could eat only dry toast, boiled chicken and mashed potatoes. He was a broken man in many ways.

When I was thirteen I left Clinton Street Public School for the summer holidays with my ruler, pen, pencil, eraser and a scribbler on the first four pages of which was an essay, *How I Will Spend My Summer Holidays.* For the next two months we were supposed to fill up the rest of the book with accounts of the fulfillment of those hopes. I left also with a certificate to take me into high school, with an attached letter from the principal indicating a great scholastic future for me. That was on the last Friday of June. On Monday I was apprenticed to a machine in a factory making ladies' hats; six months without pay, then thirty-five cents an hour if I proved myself. My father swore by the Virgin Mary and Her Son that I was sixteen and since he was an atheist he thought it was a good trick to play on the "capitalist exploiters." To me he said, If one doesn't work, one doesn't eat. Remember, you belong to the working class and nothing will ever change that. Education makes no difference: a word mispronounced, the cut of your coat, the shape of your nose — you will always reveal your class. By remaining with the proletariat you will not be tempted to falsify your life. Since he was too ill to work and too proud to go on relief, I became his surrogate in the ranks of the proletariat.

First it was the foreman, then the salesman, and ultimately my boss: by granting them small privileges — they were good family men and desired only a little titillation — I was able to make more money, get promotions, until I became, at sixteen, a forelady in the factory. In time I became experienced in matters other than millinery. Still I couldn't get away from the factory. Affairs, marriage: I had no luck with men: my father's predictions came true: I always ended up having to go back to work at a machine. So you see, for me now it is enough to live in a nice house. Where, and with whom, with love, without love, it does not matter. It is enough to live in comfort and dignity. Your husband is a kind man, never raises his voice; I always know exactly what I can count on. He asks only to be free to ride his horse on weekends. However, should you wish to resume your former place in this house, then of course I will leave. It is all the same to me; there are many lonely men in this world.

I looked at my watch. It was 6:20. I could hear water running through the pipes. The children washing up for dinner. Francesca also looked at her watch. She said, They won't come down until the very last second. I said, I know. They hate sitting down to dinner with their parents. She added, Ten minutes. We knew the reference was to Zbigniew who, at this moment, would be in the basement, polishing his boots. A tacit understanding arose between Francesca and me; we became bound by the same picture. We both saw Zbigniew at the workbench, with the cloths, brushes and polishes laid out. First he wipes off the dust and mud with an old towel. Then he dips his first two fingers into a jar of mink oil and slowly rubs the creamy substance into the leather. He waits for a little while then applies black polish. He waits another minute then vigorously shines the boots with a soft brush. Francesca said, Please stay; the children will be happy to see you. I handed her my coat, which she hung up in the hall closet. She added, I think they miss you, but I also think that they have accepted me. Their lives are unchanged.

Anton and Dina came down the stairs together, precisely at 6:30, and said, Hi Mom, in passing. Zbigniew came through the kitchen at the same time and did not notice me until we were all in the dining room. There was some hesitation where I was to sit until Zbigniew rose and brought in a chair for me and placed it to his right. On my right was Dina, Anton across the table and Francesca at my former place at the end nearest the kitchen.

– How have you been? my husband asked.

– Very well, thank you, I smiled at him, how have *you* been?

– I've had a bad cold.

Francesca, passing plates of cabbage rolls, said, I gave him a hot whisky and aspirins at night.

– That was the right thing to do, I commented: Are you over your cold?

– It hung on for weeks: it took it out of me: my routine suffered. I'm back on course now.

– Your children, Francesca addressed me, your children do not like cabbage.

Anton and Dina were suppressing laughter or rage, I could not tell. They made no noise, waiting, I knew, for the ordeal of the dinner hour to be over. Upstairs, under mattresses, was a cache of potato chips and chocolate bars. Their faces vacant, their eyes distrustful — what will become of them? I wondered.

Francesca brought in cookies and peaches for dessert. I had baked the cookies and put them in the freezer; I had canned the peaches on a hot, humid day in September. It crossed my mind that it was too soon to open the canned peaches: they were intended for mid-winter, when their taste would bring memories of summer. I thought, I do not mind you taking my place; I do not mind you feeding my children; but you have no right to take as yours the peaches I sweated over.

My anger, habitually, is wordless. Yet the children always sense what my thoughts are; and I always know that *they* know, because they have the capacity or the innocence to act out their discomfort. Anton and Dina rose together from the table, scraping their chairs (what happened to the rug?), deliberately backing away from the table in horror as if they'd been served live eels. Zbigniew laughed; and while they know it is his way of staying out of the situation, they pretended to be encouraged by his laughter. In high spirits they ran from the room. The meal ended in the silence I knew so well. I offered to do the dishes: that despised task, the washing up, was welcomed as escape. Francesca demurred, saying I was a guest after all, it was her duty, she didn't mind, it was a privilege for her, she liked things tidy. However, the old habit persisted and I picked up four, five dishes to make my exit plausible. All right, she said, but I was only to rinse and stack: she had her own system for the dishwasher.

In the kitchen, each time I turned off the tap, I could hear Francesca's voice in a light, gossipy tone telling Zbigniew something. When she came to the end of the account, there was silence again until she began another diversion. Against the silences I found relief in the familiar things around me: the patterns of the wallpaper, the patterns of the floor tiles, the patterns on the china. My hands and feet went about their kitchen business without thought on my part. There were even a few moments of pleasure as I put away knives, pots, towel, apron and broom, exactly where they were supposed to go. I worked quietly. My curiosity was aroused: he allows her to chatter, as he did me, without comment; but when he ultimately speaks, as he does just once before he goes back to his newspapers, will he reveal anything I want to know? What he tells her I have heard a thousand times.

– When I was fourteen my grandfather gave me a thoroughbred Arab mare for my birthday. She was of a breed from Hungary called Furioso. They were well named, those proud, beautiful animals. I called her Fury. She was high-tailed, white, with a silky white mane. She had wide, dark eyes, neat ears and flared nostrils. Oh but she was spirited. No one could come near her, let alone ride her. Even my grandfather, a former Cossack and cavalry officer was afraid of her. My grandfather intended to beat her into submission, but I asked for a chance to tame her. It was agreed: if I could not ride her within one week, she would be turned into a workhorse. I had one of our servants lock me in the stall with Fury. In the morning, at the first light of day, the same terrified servant opened the lock, certain he would find me trampled to death. Instead, I walked out, leading Fury, who was as submissive as a donkey. I was her master. On two occasions I raced her in Warsaw. We won. How did I subdue her? That will remain my secret forever.

– I imagine it was a matter of superior malice, Francesca said.

Her remark must have ended the table talk, for she came into the kitchen. She went around the room closing the three doors that lead into it. Zbigniew would be back in the family room with his newspapers. Francesca and I faced one another on stools at the kitchen counter.

She said   – Your summer things have been packed in marked cartons. I put white shoe polish on your sandals; they'll be ready to wear the first hot day next summer.

I said   – Those long hot days. Those long hot useless weekends.

She said   – Zbigniew is pleased that I learned to prepare Polish dishes. I can cook cabbage in many different ways — cabbage rolls, hot cabbage soup with meat or cold cabbage borscht with sour cream, coleslaw; there's a crock of cabbage in the basement for sauerkraut.

I said   – Those long hot nights. I woke in the middle of the night and went out to lie down on the deck in the garden. He didn't stir.

– I have registered for a course in French cooking. I think Zbigniew will like French cooking, the Poles and the French got along well: the French loved Chopin. Zbigniew reads Baudelaire in the original. Did you know your husband wrote a book of poems in French, *Les Illuminations d'Amour*?

– In September I drove to High Park every day. I left the car near the Bloor Street entrance and walked deep into the park. There were lovers everywhere. On the slopes in the sun, behind bushes, on top of picnic tables. They looked as if they might be foreigners. Don't misunderstand me, I mean only that, possibly, where they came from there was not that freedom to hug and kiss in the open. Perhaps there were some Canadian lovers also. I couldn't tell. I always took a book and held it open in front of me so that they wouldn't catch me staring.

– Zbigniew is so clever, he speaks eight languages and several Slavic dialects. I asked him to help me with my French, but I don't believe he has the patience to think in two languages at night when he must do that all day as a translator in the courts. He didn't say he wouldn't help me: he just didn't.

– In October the light was bright, the air dry and sharp, leaves crunched underfoot. The lovers didn't see me. They never took their eyes off one another.

– Last Thursday, Zbigniew had a particularly trying day. I read about it in the paper. The defendant was from Jugoslavia, his wife Italian and the witness, their landlady, was Portuguese. The husband was accused of keeping his wife tied to a chair, her mouth gagged, while he was at work. The landlady discovered her when she knocked on the door to borrow a cup of oil. The magistrate looked down at the wife who was seated before him on her chair, still bound and gagged. Why didn't the landlady untie her? the magistrate asked. The translator — that's Zbigniew! — said, Your Honor, she says it is dangerous to interfere in the affairs of married couples. She thinks he must have had good reason for what he did to his wife. Find out, the judge instructed, why he binds and gags his wife. Your Honor, Zbigniew said, he says he does it for her sake, for her safety. He says she comes from Genoa and goes wandering down around Toronto Harbor and talks to sailors like in the old country.

– One Sunday morning I went to the park but I didn't stay very long. It was November, the trees were bare. Dry leaves whirled and sailed in the wind. The lovers seemed obsessed: in their faces, in the way they clutched each other, was a desperation that one associates with the classic tragedies of star-crossed lovers. There were not many people about; we all seemed resigned to something; the old men to walking their dogs, the dogs resigned to the pace of the old men; the lovers to being satisfied with just a glimpse of the other's face and a touch of the hands; and I to my solitary walks. When it began to rain I took the streetcar at the Howard Park entrance, leaving the car behind. I did not go home. I walked on Yonge Street, north, on the east side, a walk I had often taken when I was young and when this part of the city was foreign to me. There was a cold drizzle. There were few pedestrians. There were some middle-aged people in Murray's out for their Sunday dinner — I could see their heads over the top of the short window curtains. The shops no longer interested me, with their pseudo-exotic displays, with their dusty shoes, with their limp clothing. A bookstore was open and for a moment I found it strange, until I remembered that the Sunday "blue" laws had changed. I went in and picked up and put down endless numbers of books. For the first time, I had no wish to read. Before I knew it, it was nine o'clock. I was cold, wet and tired, yet I still was not ready to go home. Outside, the marquee of the New Yorker Cinema shone bright against the gloom, with *Children of Paradise* in large letters. I went in.

– Zbigniew and I were alone in the living room that same evening. I asked him how the case had ended. Zbigniew said it had been such a terrible ordeal for him — instructions from the magistrate, the principals all speaking at once, the wife when untied screaming obscenities in Italian which he found difficult to translate — that he asked to be taken off the case.

– I stayed to see the film twice. I had to see again that part near the end when Garance and Baptiste embrace and she says to him, *I never forgot you. You have helped me to live through all these years. It's you who has prevented me from becoming old, and stupid, and spoiled.* And Baptiste replies, *I've thought of you every day.* Garance whispers, *My life was so empty, and I fell so alone. But I told myself,*

*You have no right to be sad, you are one of the happy ones in spite of
everything, because someone really loved you.*

– Zbigniew said that his grandfather would have known
how to deal with a wayward wife. Then he took the riding
crop off its hook at the side of the mantel and struck his palm
with it, then thrashed the air around him.

– I came home about two in the morning. The lights were
on in the living room. I glanced in before I hung up my coat.
Zbigniew was standing beside the fireplace, his hands behind
his back. He followed me up the stairs to the bedroom. In his
hand was his grandfather's riding crop, which always hangs
on a hook beside the mantel. He didn't say a word. He raised
the riding crop. I bent my head, protecting myself with my
arms.

The riding crop belonged to his grandfather, it is only a
memento. Zbigniew never uses it, not even on his horse. He
put it back on its hook.

I was afraid. At the same time I was aware of a contra-
diction: Zbigniew had often told me he would never whip
a horse. I believed him. I have never known him to lose his
temper. I used to wonder what would happen if we quarreled:
I would scream accusations at him; perhaps he would hit
me — with his hand. I could understand that. I straightened
up; I faced him.

It was only Thursday, but even so I suggested it would do
him good to relax in bed, we could make love and he would
get a good sleep. He would not make an exception. He said,
Tomorrow is a long day in court; I must get up early; I have
to have all my wits about me. He went to sleep after the ten
o'clock news as usual.

I said   – He wouldn't look at me. He struck me three times. I
felt the whip on my face, my breasts and my legs. He said

nothing. We went to bed. We had intercourse as we always do on Sunday.

She said – His refusal was not directed against me; I didn't mind. He is an honorable man — he has never taken the scissors to my credit cards, as I've heard other husbands do. I am satisfied. It is a good life, this, to live with a virtuous man.

I said – Virtue is not capacity. To you, however, I offer gratitude, if you require it. Tell me, how soon after I was gone did you move in?

– You left the door unlocked. I was here when Zbigniew got home from work.

– Then despite everything, he has been able to maintain his schedule?

– To the minute.

Again the household sounds held me. Overhead I recognized the children's quick steps; a door shut, then another. We both heard the (anticipated) click of the bathroom lock, which we knew meant that Zbigniew had started his bath. Francesca and I simultaneously glanced at the clock on the wall. A sense of communion sprang up between us, so that, in a manner of speaking, we became one mind. A nod, a glance, and wordlessly we confirmed that since it was 9:30 on a Sunday night, we, twin-like, would go up and await our husband in bed. Zbigniew's instructions, apparently have been explicit for her, too; she opened the freezer at the top of the refrigerator, took out a bottle of vodka, poured a tumbler full, replaced the bottle. She will carry the drink up to the bedroom, and when she hears the bathwater draining in the adjoining room, she will stand at the bathroom door which will open about six inches and she will put her hand holding the glass through the opening. The tumbler will be taken from her hand by his (unseen) hand. For my part, right now, temptation in the form of habit prompts me to want to take the vodka from her and carry it upstairs myself. The ennui of well-ordered events has a cozy appeal. So that when Francesca invites me to spend the night, she catches me in a hiatus of purpose. It would be a relief to fall into a familiar bed. My agreement to stay came largely from indecision.

The bedroom has been redecorated. An effect has been created of a lovers' bower, even though the point finally becomes redundant: pink roses clamber up and around blue trellises everywhere: on the walls, drapes, all over the bed on the comforter, and under one's head on the pillowcases. I think: this is as close as I'll ever come to a bed of roses. The king-size bed takes up most of the room, so that there is only the airspace overhead and a few feet here and there between dressers and night tables and bed that are free of false roses. I prefer the neutrality of stripes or geometric figures. I wondered if my toothbrush is still in its holder. I will have to wait until Zbigniew is finished to find out. It is possible I won't get a chance to brush my teeth, as so often happened on Sunday night, unless I brushed my teeth before he began his ritual for the night. I find a clean nightgown in its usual place in the left-hand corner of the bottom drawer of my dresser. When Francesca bustles in with the glass of vodka in her hand she has the look of a hospital nurse making the rounds with medications for the night. We listen to the bathwater gurgle down the drain and hear the click of the lock and see the door open slightly. Francesca puts the glass through the opening, then withdraws her hand, empty.

I lie down in my accustomed place at the side of the bed near the door, maintaining the feeling that I can slip out of bed anytime, should I find it necessary to do so for one reason or another. Francesca stands before me in one of my nightgowns that hangs on her as had the dress, straight down, without a curve anywhere. She invites me by gestures to sleep beside Zbigniew in the middle of the bed and I, also using gestures, indicate I wish to remain where I am. She comes into bed, plumps her pillow, yawns, the yawn ending in a sigh of contentment. And at that moment my unspoken question is answered: she is completely adaptable. She is not beautiful, or even handsome; her attractiveness possibly lies in a kind of simple willingness, a compliance uncluttered by second thought. Soon Zbigniew emerges in his blue velour robe. He stands at his side of the bed, his hand on the light switch. He looks in my direction, his expression not unkind, waiting, it seems, for me to say something, but waits only briefly, then he turns off the light and in the dark he removes his robe (I remember).

Zbigniew has never been seen naked. And when he gets under the cover, we three pull and tug gently at the eiderdown to divide it fairly between us. The room, however, does not remain entirely dark; he has neglected to close the Venetian blinds in the dressing room that shut out the light from the street lamp. In the dimness I can also make out the forms beside me. As I feel them stirring I wonder if he has begun to stroke her back. Even though I am (once) removed, I can smell the stables on him, a not-unpleasant odor that persists despite (his) prolonged bathing — it is an odor I have come to associate with having my legs spread by his knees and his immediate entry. The mattress heaves and I imagine that now Zbigniew is inside her. I close my eyes. Now he will roll over on his right side, remaining inside her, pinning down her left leg with his iron thigh, so that she cannot move, even if aroused. Any other touch between them will be accidental: he will not caress or kiss her. He will fuck her with slow deliberation, sometimes stopping, then starting up again. Whether my presence has increased their ardour I have no way of knowing. I notice only that the small movements and the absence of words are the same as when I lay immobilized beneath him. In visualizing them together the (persistent) image of Zbigniew on his mare crowds my mind and an anger rises: Why can't (won't?)

he be as vigorous, maintain the same stamina with Francesca as he does with his mare!

Despite myself, I am overcome by the ache of lust. The desire that comes flooding is not for Zbigniew. Behind my eyes I conjure up Coenraad. He appears before me, naked and splendid. In this big bed I can spread my legs without touching anyone. Unexpectedly, my lover's image gives way to Andy's, who also is naked and splendid. As I open for him, his figure, in turn, vanishes and I see a golden wasp enter the purple centre of an orchid. I place an arm over my eyes and put my other hand between my legs. When I come, I stifle the sound that might betray me. What is unusual is that this is the first time I have climaxed at the same time as my husband. I become aware that he has rolled away from her; we lie very still.

While Zbigniew slept, Francesca and I slipped out of bed. I left behind my basic black dress where I had tossed it earlier over the back of a chair. I picked up my pearls on the dresser. Then, on my way out I reached into the cupboard beside the door and even in that faint light I was able to put my hand on a certain silk dress, more appropriate for spring perhaps, but it was the one I wanted to take with me. I remembered it had an abstract design in slashes of red and blue and yellow on a green background, copied, I felt at the time I bought it, from the paintings of Hundertwasser. Francesca, meanwhile, of her own accord, gathered up the rest of my things. It was not very late; bands of light shone from under Dina's and Anton's doors. I paused in the hall, then, sad, I descended the stairs. In my letter I will try and explain why I could not stop to kiss them good-night.

Francesca, handing me my coat in the hall, said,

– You need have no jealousy; I never have an orgasm.

– Just the same, I said, I must leave. Would you like my pearls? She held the strand up to the light.

– They're beautiful. Thank you.

– You must understand I no longer belong here.

– Yes, of course. I'll call a cab. I hope you know what you're doing — you'll never find another man as decent as your husband.

– Empty virtue repels me.

– You would think twice if you knew the world as I know it.

For the first time in this house I laughed out loud.

My driver remarked that he liked Yonge Street on Sunday night because there was hardly any traffic. He sat at the wheel with his head tipped back slightly to let me know, I guessed, he would listen to me. I huddled in the right-hand corner of the backseat, unable to say a word. At Castlefield, I could tell he gave up expecting anything from me because he leaned straight forward over the wheel. There was no activity on the streets; the small shops were closed, only the billboards were bright; and, at Bloor, *Children of Paradise* was still spelled out on the marquee. Tonight the invisible multitude behind closed doors were putting in time somehow until they could stream out into the streets and roads on Monday morning. As we taxied across town, I thought: out there the city goes on being the city, more or less seductive, more or less comforting. In this city, I decided, I will continue to walk: walk beside the lake, walk along the old streets, walk into new neighbourhoods, noting the ways of people, keeping my step light. But I won't be trying to recognize my lover.

I think I will miss Coenraad. I will miss the joy when he appears; I will not miss the pain of our partings.

And I will miss airports. Even though all time is dead time until the gates open; even though waiting for my plane an hour, or six hours, I become like a lung fish sealed in mud in the dry season; even though I revive only when my flight is called — I will miss the anticipation of getting on a plane that takes me to

Coenraad. I will miss the ride in from the airport, wanting to look at both sides of the road at once, seeing houses different from any I've ever seen before. I will miss the fascination of a strange city, especially when it appears below me at night like another firmament ablaze with synthetic stars.

Most of all I will miss railway stations in the morning, the first rays of the sun creating faint shadows, or, in the gray north, no shadows at all; the vast domed palaces with numbered tracks, the old iron horses snorting steam; the food kiosks, red wine from a barrel, baguettes and cheeses; porters, vendors, women and children, baggage carts, loudspeakers; all, all under an eerie green light giving the feeling that last night's dream had begun again; the tears, the smiles, the elderly too early for their train; a child's abandoned teddy bear on a bench.

I will not miss being a stranger from whom nothing is wanted and from whom nothing is expected.

The click and scrape of the windshield wipers brought me back. A snowstorm had come up; heavy white flakes were being driven against the headlights. We were on Elm Street. Before long I saw Andy's attic, lit up, the glass eaves glowing yellow against the night. I felt like a gambler who finds in another pocket a few forgotten coins that will keep him in the game. Stop here, I said. I waited for a few moments. Then I felt something like resolve grow in me, a resolve against waiting. There will be risks. I paid the fare, crossed the street and began walking. The air felt good. I remembered that the air always changed with the first snowfall. I was cold in my thin spring dress and light coat, but for once I didn't have far to walk.

AFTERWORD

WHEN I FIRST read Helen Weinzweig's *Basic Black with Pearls* several years ago, I emerged in the sort of daze that happens when a book seems to ferret out your most secret thoughts and hopes. Since then I've described the book to others as an "interior feminist espionage novel." That is, of course, a reductive way to look at this work, which is so much more than that single phrase can express. And yet those four words, taken together, suggest the scope and the breadth, the daring and the audacity, the humor and the pathos contained in a work of less than one hundred and fifty pages. It was a novel I did not know I was looking for, but finding it was a revelation.

The interior nature of *Basic Black* is central to its unfolding. Shirley Kaszenbowski, regarded from the outside, is the embodiment of the "invisible woman." She is in her early forties, long-married with two children. She wanders through Toronto in the titular basic black dress, a strand of pearls around her neck, cloaked by a tweed coat—designed to last for decades—from the city's most expensive, most fashionable, and snobbiest department store. "I fool no one," Shirley admits. "I am regarded as a woman with no apparent purpose, offering no reason for my presence." Regarded from inside, however, Shirley is anything but purposeless. She is aglow. Her appearance, her age, her station is a cloak for a rich life of travel, adventure, and meaning. As the critic Art Seidenbaum noted in his review for the *Los Angeles Times*, "her odyssey is erotic, but her appearance is prosaic."

What seems like aimless shopping and fruitless wandering is cover for Shirley's ongoing search for her lover, Coenraad. He fills her with a sense of longing and purpose that her husband, Zbigniew, cannot: "When I see that stance of Coenraad's all fears disappear: babies don't die, cars don't collide, planes fly on course, muzak is silenced, certitude reigns. That is how I always recognize my love: the way he stands, the way I feel." By contrast, Zbigniew's weekly routine conjures up an opposite image: "I was thinking particularly of Sundays at home when Zbigniew comes back from the stables, hangs up his riding crop beside the mantel-piece and settles in with the week's newspapers." So long have Sundays made Shirley shudder that adultery is a refuge.

Then again, we only have Shirley's word for what's happened. That uncertainty will prove critical later.

Masks and costumes suffuse the narrative of *Basic Black with Pearls*. Shirley's exterior life as a housewife and mother is also a disguise, which is why it's critical to look at the "feminist" and "espionage" parts in tandem.

Basic Black with Pearls contains overt references to Virginia Woolf and covert ones to feminist classics like Kate Chopin's *The Awakening* and Charlotte Perkins Gilman's "The Yellow Wall-paper." The scholar Ruth Panofsky, who wrote extensively about Weinzweig, sees echoes of George Eliot. Others have compared Weinzweig to the Canadian Margarets: Laurence and Atwood. I, however, see resonances and overtones in a novel published eight years after *Basic Black*: David Markson's *Wittgenstein's Mistress*. Weinzweig kept a copy of Markson's 1988 novel in her personal library, which makes me think she recognized some kinship with her own work. (Whether Markson read Weinzweig is less clear.)

These novels describe women not only breaking away from conventions, but also filled with desire and ambition that are almost too much to bear, a secret from themselves. Weinzweig had to search out these books to counteract decades of reading male-dominated narratives, which she needed to reject to construct her own style. "One of the things I had to learn after reading all this male fiction was, what do I as a woman feel like," she said in a 1990 interview. "All the literary forms were men's, all the philosophies were men's philosophies. . . . I had to translate these forms into the female."

Shirley's lover, Coenraad, appears to be some kind of spy with a nebulous organization known as "The Agency." Often Shirley meets him—in Vienna, Paris, or closer to home. "Coenraad and I have a code for our meetings, taking the printed word and interpreting it according to mathematical formulae." A specific volume of *National Geographic* is equal parts clue and inspiration.

Coenraad, at nearly every turn, wears a disguise, cloaking his face, his manner. He appears as a "downtown wino," a "derelict in prop clothes, in a stained green jacket, too long in the sleeves, loose trousers held up somehow." They don't speak much in public because "he must be on the *qui vive* at all times, and I because his presence renders me speechless."

Shirley, too, adopts disguises. Her married name of Kaszenbowski supersedes her maiden name of Silverberg. She also takes on the name "Lola Montez"—the pseudonym for the real-life Victorian-era ballet dancer and actress Maria Dolores Eliza Rosanna Gilbert—when checking into hotels for her latest assignation with Coenraad. Weinzweig uses humor as a cudgel, a tension breaker, a means of complicating the narrative. Humor also deflects attention from the woman underneath Shirley's oh-so-proper costume. Zbigniew's rigid Sunday routine fills her with dread, and yet, moments after identifying her revulsion, Shirley thinks: "I live in a nice house, you know. My house is in a nice part of Toronto. I hate disorder. . . . I miss putting things in order."

This vacillation between order and chaos at home hints at Shirley's greatest mask: sanity. *Basic Black with Pearls* dances on the edge of it, leaving the reader to wonder whether madness, be it schizophrenia or some other disorder, may be the most logical explanation of the story she is trying to tell. (At one point she discovers Zbigniew reading a newspaper article about her admittance to a hospital: "She claimed to have neither husband, children or other family; nor did she have a family physician.")

Weinzweig, however, is too astute to slide into platitudes when there are more pressing liminal spaces to mine. "It seems to me that in a confusion of extremes one either lies or tells the truth, whichever works best," Shirley says. "Up until now the risk of deceit has, for me, been greater than the risk of truth."

Basic Black with Pearls, upon its publication in 1980, was greeted with a mix of praise and misunderstanding. Critics sensed its daring and applauded its formal inventiveness, but those qualities also kept people at bay. One newspaper review from my hometown of Ottawa, Canada, castigated the novel for being "a writer's book, not a reader's book," the "illegitimate offspring of Franz Kafka," and "too good to accommodate the present level of Canadian culture." In other words, CanLit wasn't supposed to be written this way.

In fact, Weinzweig didn't draw on Canadian literature, largely preferring European writers, often not of prose. She had previously published several short stories and a novel, *Passing Ceremony*

(1973). Ostensibly about a wedding and the guests in attendance, *Passing Ceremony* is far more about the nature of coupling and decoupling and the madness and anxiety that exists in between those two states. Weinzweig drew from the work of Alain Robbe-Grillet, Samuel Beckett, and Nathalie Sarraute for the short prose sections, some as short as a single line.

Mid-twentieth-century European literature does not provide the entire answer to the question of influence. Weinzweig's Jewish upbringing is part of the equation as well. She told her original book editor to read *The Joys of Yiddish*; the mourner's Kaddish is directly referenced in *Basic Black with Pearls*.

The jagged rhythm of *Passing Ceremony* and *Basic Black with Pearls* also owes much to the work of Helen's husband, John Weinzweig, arguably Canada's most important native-born composer of classical music. Their marriage was, for decades, not one of equals. At first Helen stuck to traditional roles of muse, helpmeet, mother of sons, housewife. John was the creative force, the one whose art needed the space for nurturing. ("Both John and I lived his career," she once said.) What free time she had she devoted to volunteering—as chaperon to the country's National Youth Orchestra, as an overseer of a cooperative nursery school—and to reading widely and obsessively.

These were roles Helen sought out as an escape from a childhood of dislocation and trauma, beginning with emigration from Poland at age nine, being raised by a single mother thereafter in a poor Jewish neighborhood in Toronto (since heavily gentrified and christened the Annex), and a two-year sanatorium stint while recovering from tuberculosis (where she picked up her voracious reading habit in earnest). A reunion at age seventeen with her estranged father, in Milan, was so disastrous it might better be described as a kidnapping. He didn't allow her to leave for months. She never saw him again. Weinzweig transformed her harrowing experience into one of the most uncanny and original moments in *Basic Black with Pearls*. In a scene set at the Art Gallery of Ontario, Shirley is so overcome by the bold colors and figures of Pierre Bonnard's painting *Dining Room on the Garden* that she enters into communion with its pained female subject, who seems to merge into the wall behind her and who cries to Shirley, "I am a prisoner of my mad father!"

Marrying John, whom Helen first knew in high school, hinted at a solution to the problem of her youth, as she explained in a 1985 interview.

> I grew up without a sense of family. Other people had families. So when I married and had my own family, I think I tried to create a family life out of my head. I feel I failed. I still don't know, in other than an intellectual way, what makes a family. So the "sense" of family creeps into my work in a negative way, i.e., what is wrong with this or that family.... I chose the traditional route of marriage and motherhood because I wanted to be accepted by the world around me. Why that was so had a lot to do with my mother. She refused to follow the path of other women.... I decided I would be respectable, and became more so than Caesar's wife.

The costume of respectability turned out to have an expiry date. At forty-five—roughly the same age as Shirley—Helen became depressed and had difficulty reading. With a therapist's help, she turned to writing. Weinzweig's success rate at placing short stories with publications was remarkably high, perhaps because her voice, which mixed mirth and myrrh, shone through from the first.

"The Care and Feeding of Canadian Composers," one of Helen's first published works, appears on the surface to be a gentle but affectionate mocking of her life with John. The bird motifs abound. Everyone can sit around and laugh. But the melancholy air lingers around phrases like "His occupation is a solitary one, but he does not like to live alone" or "The Canadian composer is usually a mild-mannered duck, but can easily turn into a tight-lipped grouse."

The feeling of pointed melancholy in Weinzweig's work made more sense to me after I spent a recent afternoon sifting through a selection of her voluminous personal journals, part of her archives at the University of Toronto. In typewritten missives spanning from the early 1960s through the early 2000s, Weinzweig chronicled dreams and desires, frustrations and hopes, affairs of long and fleeting duration—all of the fertile stuff that creates the unconscious mind that is necessary for creative output. Extended correspondence with one lover, a former board trustee for a Washington, D.C.–based university whom she first met in New York and whom she would see sporadically for decades, strongly hints at the inspiration for Coenraad.

Yet Weinzweig's output was sparse: two novels, a short-story collection (*A View from the Roof*, 1989), several plays, and a few pieces of nonfiction, before dementia took her mind years before her death in 2010 at age ninety-four. She once said that a good writing year produced twenty publishable pages. No wonder *Basic Black* took six years to complete.

A novel needs an ending, but *Basic Black with Pearls* manages to subvert that requirement, too. Shirley, through with her interior wanderings and fruitless search for Coenraad, returns to her Toronto home. To her husband, Zbigniew, the type of man who "didn't say he wouldn't help me: he just didn't," who sticks with a regular, rigid routine. To her children, Anton and Dina. And to the recesses of her mind, fractured, perhaps, by schizophrenia and multiple hospitalizations. Upon arrival, Shirley meets Francesca. Her double, her twin, her replacement.

There is no jealousy on Shirley's part, only relief. There is a thrilling, disturbing ménage à trois scene that is far more nurturing than erotic. And then Shirley disappears again, towards a new lover, taking flight from the trappings of domesticity as well as the intoxication of pure freedom. Towards a place where she "will not miss being a stranger from whom nothing is wanted and from whom nothing is expected."

Weinzweig struggled with the ending of *Basic Black with Pearls* for more than a year. "I could find no solution for this woman who leaves home—whether she leaves home physically or mentally is not the point," she said in a 1982 interview. "But she does leave her occupation, which is wife and mother, and goes out into the big world. And I couldn't find anything for her to do out in that big world. That question has disturbed me as a person and as a writer."

No doubt Weinzweig's discomfort stemmed as much from what the ending said about women of a certain age as it said about her own life. Is Shirley succumbing to a similar, moralistic fate that affects the younger, flightier Marjorie Morningstar, of Herman Wouk's novel published a generation earlier?

I see it a little differently. Liberation is a process, a continuum, where choices can be permanent but are more often permeable. Wherever Shirley Kaszenbowski goes, whatever decisions she makes, her mind remains alive. The possibilities are without limits because they aren't constrained by reality. She isn't a cautionary tale or a trauma case in that costume of black dress and pearl necklace. She, like her creator and avatar, is a marvel.

—SARAH WEINMAN

TITLES IN SERIES

For a complete list of titles, visit www.nyrb.com or write to:
Catalog Requests, NYRB, 435 Hudson Street, New York, NY 10014

J.R. ACKERLEY Hindoo Holiday*
J.R. ACKERLEY My Dog Tulip*
J.R. ACKERLEY My Father and Myself*
J.R. ACKERLEY We Think the World of You*
HENRY ADAMS The Jeffersonian Transformation
RENATA ADLER Pitch Dark*
RENATA ADLER Speedboat*
AESCHYLUS Prometheus Bound; translated by Joel Agee*
LEOPOLDO ALAS His Only Son *with* Doña Berta*
CÉLESTE ALBARET Monsieur Proust
DANTE ALIGHIERI The Inferno
KINGSLEY AMIS The Alteration*
KINGSLEY AMIS Dear Illusion: Collected Stories*
KINGSLEY AMIS Ending Up*
KINGSLEY AMIS Girl, 20*
KINGSLEY AMIS The Green Man*
KINGSLEY AMIS Lucky Jim*
KINGSLEY AMIS The Old Devils*
KINGSLEY AMIS One Fat Englishman*
KINGSLEY AMIS Take a Girl Like You*
ROBERTO ARLT The Seven Madmen*
U.R. ANANTHAMURTHY Samskara: A Rite for a Dead Man*
WILLIAM ATTAWAY Blood on the Forge
W.H. AUDEN (EDITOR) The Living Thoughts of Kierkegaard
W.H. AUDEN W. H. Auden's Book of Light Verse
ERICH AUERBACH Dante: Poet of the Secular World
EVE BABITZ Eve's Hollywood*
EVE BABITZ Slow Days, Fast Company: The World, the Flesh, and L.A.*
DOROTHY BAKER Cassandra at the Wedding*
DOROTHY BAKER Young Man with a Horn*
J.A. BAKER The Peregrine
S. JOSEPHINE BAKER Fighting for Life*
HONORÉ DE BALZAC The Human Comedy: Selected Stories*
HONORÉ DE BALZAC The Memoirs of Two Young Wives*
HONORÉ DE BALZAC The Unknown Masterpiece *and* Gambara*
VICKI BAUM Grand Hotel*
SYBILLE BEDFORD A Favorite of the Gods *and* A Compass Error*
SYBILLE BEDFORD A Legacy*
SYBILLE BEDFORD A Visit to Don Otavio: A Mexican Journey*
MAX BEERBOHM The Prince of Minor Writers: The Selected Essays of Max Beerbohm*
MAX BEERBOHM Seven Men
STEPHEN BENATAR Wish Her Safe at Home*
FRANS G. BENGTSSON The Long Ships*
ALEXANDER BERKMAN Prison Memoirs of an Anarchist
GEORGES BERNANOS Mouchette
MIRON BIAŁOSZEWSKI A Memoir of the Warsaw Uprising*
ADOLFO BIOY CASARES Asleep in the Sun

* *Also available as an electronic book.*

ADOLFO BIOY CASARES The Invention of Morel
PAUL BLACKBURN (TRANSLATOR) Proensa*
CAROLINE BLACKWOOD Corrigan*
CAROLINE BLACKWOOD Great Granny Webster*
RONALD BLYTHE Akenfield: Portrait of an English Village*
NICOLAS BOUVIER The Way of the World
EMMANUEL BOVE Henri Duchemin and His Shadows*
MALCOLM BRALY On the Yard*
MILLEN BRAND The Outward Room*
ROBERT BRESSON Notes on the Cinematograph*
SIR THOMAS BROWNE Religio Medici and Urne-Buriall*
JOHN HORNE BURNS The Gallery
ROBERT BURTON The Anatomy of Melancholy
MATEI CALINESCU The Life and Opinions of Zacharias Lichter*
CAMARA LAYE The Radiance of the King
GIROLAMO CARDANO The Book of My Life
DON CARPENTER Hard Rain Falling*
J.L. CARR A Month in the Country*
LEONORA CARRINGTON Down Below*
BLAISE CENDRARS Moravagine
EILEEN CHANG Little Reunions*
EILEEN CHANG Love in a Fallen City*
EILEEN CHANG Naked Earth*
JOAN CHASE During the Reign of the Queen of Persia*
ELLIOTT CHAZE Black Wings Has My Angel*
UPAMANYU CHATTERJEE English, August: An Indian Story
RENÉ-FRANÇOIS DE CHATEAUBRIAND Memoirs from Beyond the Grave, 1768–1800
NIRAD C. CHAUDHURI The Autobiography of an Unknown Indian
ANTON CHEKHOV Peasants and Other Stories
ANTON CHEKHOV The Prank: The Best of Young Chekhov*
GABRIEL CHEVALLIER Fear: A Novel of World War I*
JEAN-PAUL CLÉBERT Paris Vagabond*
RICHARD COBB Paris and Elsewhere
COLETTE The Pure and the Impure
JOHN COLLIER Fancies and Goodnights
CARLO COLLODI The Adventures of Pinocchio*
D.G. COMPTON The Continuous Katherine Mortenhoe
IVY COMPTON-BURNETT A House and Its Head
IVY COMPTON-BURNETT Manservant and Maidservant
BARBARA COMYNS The Juniper Tree*
BARBARA COMYNS Our Spoons Came from Woolworths*
BARBARA COMYNS The Vet's Daughter
ALBERT COSSERY The Jokers*
ALBERT COSSERY Proud Beggars*
HAROLD CRUSE The Crisis of the Negro Intellectual
ASTOLPHE DE CUSTINE Letters from Russia*
LORENZO DA PONTE Memoirs
ELIZABETH DAVID A Book of Mediterranean Food
ELIZABETH DAVID Summer Cooking
L.J. DAVIS A Meaningful Life*
AGNES DE MILLE Dance to the Piper*
VIVANT DENON No Tomorrow/Point de lendemain
MARIA DERMOÛT The Ten Thousand Things

DER NISTER The Family Mashber

TIBOR DÉRY Niki: The Story of a Dog

ANTONIO DI BENEDETTO Zama*

ALFRED DÖBLIN Berlin Alexanderplatz*

ALFRED DÖBLIN Bright Magic: Stories*

JEAN D'ORMESSON The Glory of the Empire: A Novel, A History*

ARTHUR CONAN DOYLE The Exploits and Adventures of Brigadier Gerard

CHARLES DUFF A Handbook on Hanging

BRUCE DUFFY The World As I Found It*

DAPHNE DU MAURIER Don't Look Now: Stories

ELAINE DUNDY The Dud Avocado*

ELAINE DUNDY The Old Man and Me*

G.B. EDWARDS The Book of Ebenezer Le Page*

JOHN EHLE The Land Breakers*

MARCELLUS EMANTS A Posthumous Confession

EURIPIDES Grief Lessons: Four Plays; translated by Anne Carson

J.G. FARRELL Troubles*

J.G. FARRELL The Siege of Krishnapur*

J.G. FARRELL The Singapore Grip*

ELIZA FAY Original Letters from India

KENNETH FEARING The Big Clock

KENNETH FEARING Clark Gifford's Body

FÉLIX FÉNÉON Novels in Three Lines*

M.I. FINLEY The World of Odysseus

THOMAS FLANAGAN The Year of the French*

BENJAMIN FONDANE Existential Monday: Philosophical Essays*

SANFORD FRIEDMAN Conversations with Beethoven*

SANFORD FRIEDMAN Totempole*

MARC FUMAROLI When the World Spoke French

CARLO EMILIO GADDA That Awful Mess on the Via Merulana

BENITO PÉREZ GÁLDOS Tristana*

MAVIS GALLANT The Cost of Living: Early and Uncollected Stories*

MAVIS GALLANT Paris Stories*

MAVIS GALLANT A Fairly Good Time *with* Green Water, Green Sky*

MAVIS GALLANT Varieties of Exile*

GABRIEL GARCÍA MÁRQUEZ Clandestine in Chile: The Adventures of Miguel Littín

LEONARD GARDNER Fat City*

WILLIAM H. GASS In the Heart of the Heart of the Country: And Other Stories*

WILLIAM H. GASS On Being Blue: A Philosophical Inquiry*

THÉOPHILE GAUTIER My Fantoms

GE FEI The Invisibility Cloak

JEAN GENET Prisoner of Love

ÉLISABETH GILLE The Mirador: Dreamed Memories of Irène Némirovsky by Her Daughter*

NATALIA GINZBURG Family Lexicon*

JEAN GIONO Hill*

JEAN GIONO Melville: A Novel*

JOHN GLASSCO Memoirs of Montparnasse*

P.V. GLOB The Bog People: Iron-Age Man Preserved

NIKOLAI GOGOL Dead Souls*

EDMOND AND JULES DE GONCOURT Pages from the Goncourt Journals

ALICE GOODMAN History Is Our Mother: Three Libretti*

PAUL GOODMAN Growing Up Absurd: Problems of Youth in the Organized Society*

EDWARD GOREY (EDITOR) The Haunted Looking Glass

JEREMIAS GOTTHELF The Black Spider*
A.C. GRAHAM Poems of the Late T'ang
JULIEN GRACQ Balcony in the Forest*
HENRY GREEN Back*
HENRY GREEN Blindness*
HENRY GREEN Caught*
HENRY GREEN Doting*
HENRY GREEN Living*
HENRY GREEN Loving*
HENRY GREEN Nothing*
HENRY GREEN Party Going*
WILLIAM LINDSAY GRESHAM Nightmare Alley*
HANS HERBERT GRIMM Schlump*
EMMETT GROGAN Ringolevio: A Life Played for Keeps
VASILY GROSSMAN An Armenian Sketchbook*
VASILY GROSSMAN Everything Flows*
VASILY GROSSMAN Life and Fate*
VASILY GROSSMAN The Road*
LOUIS GUILLOUX Blood Dark*
OAKLEY HALL Warlock
PATRICK HAMILTON The Slaves of Solitude*
PATRICK HAMILTON Twenty Thousand Streets Under the Sky*
PETER HANDKE Short Letter, Long Farewell
PETER HANDKE Slow Homecoming
THORKILD HANSEN Arabia Felix: The Danish Expedition of 1761–1767*
ELIZABETH HARDWICK The Collected Essays of Elizabeth Hardwick*
ELIZABETH HARDWICK The New York Stories of Elizabeth Hardwick*
ELIZABETH HARDWICK Seduction and Betrayal*
ELIZABETH HARDWICK Sleepless Nights*
L.P. HARTLEY Eustace and Hilda: A Trilogy*
L.P. HARTLEY The Go-Between*
NATHANIEL HAWTHORNE Twenty Days with Julian & Little Bunny by Papa
ALFRED HAYES In Love*
ALFRED HAYES My Face for the World to See*
PAUL HAZARD The Crisis of the European Mind: 1680–1715*
ALICE HERDAN-ZUCKMAYER The Farm in the Green Mountains*
GILBERT HIGHET Poets in a Landscape
RUSSELL HOBAN Turtle Diary*
JANET HOBHOUSE The Furies
YOEL HOFFMANN The Sound of the One Hand: 281 Zen Koans with Answers*
HUGO VON HOFMANNSTHAL The Lord Chandos Letter*
JAMES HOGG The Private Memoirs and Confessions of a Justified Sinner
RICHARD HOLMES Shelley: The Pursuit*
ALISTAIR HORNE A Savage War of Peace: Algeria 1954–1962*
GEOFFREY HOUSEHOLD Rogue Male*
WILLIAM DEAN HOWELLS Indian Summer
BOHUMIL HRABAL Dancing Lessons for the Advanced in Age*
BOHUMIL HRABAL The Little Town Where Time Stood Still*
DOROTHY B. HUGHES The Expendable Man*
DOROTHY B. HUGHES In a Lonely Place*
RICHARD HUGHES A High Wind in Jamaica*
RICHARD HUGHES In Hazard*
RICHARD HUGHES The Fox in the Attic (The Human Predicament, Vol. 1)*

RICHARD HUGHES The Wooden Shepherdess (The Human Predicament, Vol. 2)*
INTIZAR HUSAIN Basti*
MAUDE HUTCHINS Victorine
YASUSHI INOUE Tun-huang*
HENRY JAMES The Ivory Tower
HENRY JAMES The New York Stories of Henry James*
HENRY JAMES The Other House
HENRY JAMES The Outcry
TOVE JANSSON Fair Play *
TOVE JANSSON The Summer Book*
TOVE JANSSON The True Deceiver*
TOVE JANSSON The Woman Who Borrowed Memories: Selected Stories*
RANDALL JARRELL (EDITOR) Randall Jarrell's Book of Stories
DAVID JONES In Parenthesis
JOSEPH JOUBERT The Notebooks of Joseph Joubert; translated by Paul Auster
KABIR Songs of Kabir; translated by Arvind Krishna Mehrotra*
FRIGYES KARINTHY A Journey Round My Skull
ERICH KÄSTNER Going to the Dogs: The Story of a Moralist*
HELEN KELLER The World I Live In
YASHAR KEMAL Memed, My Hawk
YASHAR KEMAL They Burn the Thistles
WALTER KEMPOWSKI All for Nothing
MURRAY KEMPTON Part of Our Time: Some Ruins and Monuments of the Thirties*
RAYMOND KENNEDY Ride a Cockhorse*
DAVID KIDD Peking Story*
ROBERT KIRK The Secret Commonwealth of Elves, Fauns, and Fairies
ARUN KOLATKAR Jejuri
DEZSŐ KOSZTOLÁNYI Skylark*
TÉTÉ-MICHEL KPOMASSIE An African in Greenland
GYULA KRÚDY The Adventures of Sindbad*
GYULA KRÚDY Sunflower*
SIGIZMUND KRZHIZHANOVSKY Autobiography of a Corpse*
SIGIZMUND KRZHIZHANOVSKY The Letter Killers Club*
SIGIZMUND KRZHIZHANOVSKY Memories of the Future
SIGIZMUND KRZHIZHANOVSKY The Return of Munchausen
K'UNG SHANG-JEN The Peach Blossom Fan*
GIUSEPPE TOMASI DI LAMPEDUSA The Professor and the Siren
GERT LEDIG The Stalin Front*
MARGARET LEECH Reveille in Washington: 1860–1865*
PATRICK LEIGH FERMOR Between the Woods and the Water*
PATRICK LEIGH FERMOR The Broken Road*
PATRICK LEIGH FERMOR Mani: Travels in the Southern Peloponnese*
PATRICK LEIGH FERMOR Roumeli: Travels in Northern Greece*
PATRICK LEIGH FERMOR A Time of Gifts*
PATRICK LEIGH FERMOR A Time to Keep Silence*
PATRICK LEIGH FERMOR The Traveller's Tree*
PATRICK LEIGH FERMOR The Violins of Saint-Jacques*
D.B. WYNDHAM LEWIS AND CHARLES LEE (EDITORS) The Stuffed Owl
SIMON LEYS The Death of Napoleon*
SIMON LEYS The Hall of Uselessness: Collected Essays*
GEORG CHRISTOPH LICHTENBERG The Waste Books
JAKOV LIND Soul of Wood and Other Stories
H.P. LOVECRAFT AND OTHERS Shadows of Carcosa: Tales of Cosmic Horror*

DWIGHT MACDONALD Masscult and Midcult: Essays Against the American Grain*
CURZIO MALAPARTE Kaputt
CURZIO MALAPARTE The Skin
JANET MALCOLM In the Freud Archives
JEAN-PATRICK MANCHETTE Fatale*
JEAN-PATRICK MANCHETTE The Mad and the Bad*
OSIP MANDELSTAM The Selected Poems of Osip Mandelstam
OLIVIA MANNING Fortunes of War: The Balkan Trilogy*
OLIVIA MANNING Fortunes of War: The Levant Trilogy*
OLIVIA MANNING School for Love*
JAMES VANCE MARSHALL Walkabout*
GUY DE MAUPASSANT Afloat
GUY DE MAUPASSANT Alien Hearts*
GUY DE MAUPASSANT Like Death*
JAMES McCOURT Mawrdew Czgowchwz*
WILLIAM McPHERSON Testing the Current*
MEZZ MEZZROW AND BERNARD WOLFE Really the Blues*
HENRI MICHAUX Miserable Miracle
JESSICA MITFORD Hons and Rebels
JESSICA MITFORD Poison Penmanship*
NANCY MITFORD Frederick the Great*
NANCY MITFORD Madame de Pompadour*
NANCY MITFORD The Sun King*
NANCY MITFORD Voltaire in Love*
PATRICK MODIANO In the Café of Lost Youth*
PATRICK MODIANO Young Once*
MICHEL DE MONTAIGNE Shakespeare's Montaigne; translated by John Florio*
HENRY DE MONTHERLANT Chaos and Night
BRIAN MOORE The Lonely Passion of Judith Hearne*
BRIAN MOORE The Mangan Inheritance*
ALBERTO MORAVIA Agostino*
ALBERTO MORAVIA Boredom*
ALBERTO MORAVIA Contempt*
JAN MORRIS Conundrum*
JAN MORRIS Hav*
PENELOPE MORTIMER The Pumpkin Eater*
GUIDO MORSELLI The Communist*
ÁLVARO MUTIS The Adventures and Misadventures of Maqroll
L.H. MYERS The Root and the Flower*
NESCIO Amsterdam Stories*
DARCY O'BRIEN A Way of Life, Like Any Other
SILVINA OCAMPO Thus Were Their Faces*
YURI OLESHA Envy*
IONA AND PETER OPIE The Lore and Language of Schoolchildren
IRIS OWENS After Claude*
RUSSELL PAGE The Education of a Gardener
ALEXANDROS PAPADIAMANTIS The Murderess
BORIS PASTERNAK, MARINA TSVETAYEVA, AND RAINER MARIA RILKE Letters, Summer 1926
CESARE PAVESE The Moon and the Bonfires
CESARE PAVESE The Selected Works of Cesare Pavese
BORISLAV PEKIĆ Houses*
ELEANOR PERÉNYI More Was Lost: A Memoir*
LUIGI PIRANDELLO The Late Mattia Pascal

JOSEP PLA The Gray Notebook

DAVID PLANTE Difficult Women: A Memoir of Three*

ANDREY PLATONOV The Foundation Pit

ANDREY PLATONOV Happy Moscow

ANDREY PLATONOV Soul and Other Stories

NORMAN PODHORETZ Making It*

J.F. POWERS Morte d'Urban*

J.F. POWERS The Stories of J.F. Powers*

J.F. POWERS Wheat That Springeth Green*

CHRISTOPHER PRIEST Inverted World*

BOLESŁAW PRUS The Doll*

GEORGE PSYCHOUNDAKIS The Cretan Runner: His Story of the German Occupation*

ALEXANDER PUSHKIN The Captain's Daughter*

QIU MIAOJIN Last Words from Montmartre*

QIU MIAOJIN Notes of a Crocodile*

RAYMOND QUENEAU We Always Treat Women Too Well

RAYMOND QUENEAU Witch Grass

RAYMOND RADIGUET Count d'Orgel's Ball

PAUL RADIN Primitive Man as Philosopher*

FRIEDRICH RECK Diary of a Man in Despair*

JULES RENARD Nature Stories*

JEAN RENOIR Renoir, My Father

GREGOR VON REZZORI An Ermine in Czernopol*

GREGOR VON REZZORI Memoirs of an Anti-Semite*

GREGOR VON REZZORI The Snows of Yesteryear: Portraits for an Autobiography*

TIM ROBINSON Stones of Aran: Labyrinth

TIM ROBINSON Stones of Aran: Pilgrimage

MILTON ROKEACH The Three Christs of Ypsilanti*

FR. ROLFE Hadrian the Seventh

GILLIAN ROSE Love's Work

LINDA ROSENKRANTZ Talk*

WILLIAM ROUGHEAD Classic Crimes

CONSTANCE ROURKE American Humor: A Study of the National Character

SAKI The Unrest-Cure and Other Stories; illustrated by Edward Gorey

UMBERTO SABA Ernesto*

JOAN SALES Uncertain Glory*

TAYEB SALIH Season of Migration to the North

TAYEB SALIH The Wedding of Zein*

JEAN-PAUL SARTRE We Have Only This Life to Live: Selected Essays. 1939–1975

ARTHUR SCHNITZLER Late Fame*

GERSHOM SCHOLEM Walter Benjamin: The Story of a Friendship*

DANIEL PAUL SCHREBER Memoirs of My Nervous Illness

JAMES SCHUYLER Alfred and Guinevere

JAMES SCHUYLER What's for Dinner?*

SIMONE SCHWARZ-BART The Bridge of Beyond*

LEONARDO SCIASCIA The Day of the Owl

LEONARDO SCIASCIA Equal Danger

LEONARDO SCIASCIA The Moro Affair

LEONARDO SCIASCIA To Each His Own

LEONARDO SCIASCIA The Wine-Dark Sea

VICTOR SEGALEN René Leys*

ANNA SEGHERS Transit*

PHILIPE-PAUL DE SÉGUR Defeat: Napoleon's Russian Campaign

GILBERT SELDES The Stammering Century*

VICTOR SERGE The Case of Comrade Tulayev*

VICTOR SERGE Conquered City*

VICTOR SERGE Memoirs of a Revolutionary

VICTOR SERGE Midnight in the Century*

VICTOR SERGE Unforgiving Years

SHCHEDRIN The Golovlyov Family

ROBERT SHECKLEY The Store of the Worlds: The Stories of Robert Sheckley*

GEORGES SIMENON Act of Passion*

GEORGES SIMENON Monsieur Monde Vanishes*

GEORGES SIMENON Pedigree*

GEORGES SIMENON Three Bedrooms in Manhattan*

GEORGES SIMENON Tropic Moon*

GEORGES SIMENON The Widow*

CHARLES SIMIC Dime-Store Alchemy: The Art of Joseph Cornell

MAY SINCLAIR Mary Olivier: A Life*

WILLIAM SLOANE The Rim of Morning: Two Tales of Cosmic Horror*

SASHA SOKOLOV A School for Fools*

VLADIMIR SOROKIN Ice Trilogy*

VLADIMIR SOROKIN The Queue

NATSUME SŌSEKI The Gate*

DAVID STACTON The Judges of the Secret Court*

JEAN STAFFORD The Mountain Lion

CHRISTINA STEAD Letty Fox: Her Luck

RICHARD STERN Other Men's Daughters

GEORGE R. STEWART Names on the Land

STENDHAL The Life of Henry Brulard

ADALBERT STIFTER Rock Crystal*

THEODOR STORM The Rider on the White Horse

JEAN STROUSE Alice James: A Biography*

HOWARD STURGIS Belchamber

ITALO SVEVO As a Man Grows Older

HARVEY SWADOS Nights in the Gardens of Brooklyn

A.J.A. SYMONS The Quest for Corvo

MAGDA SZABÓ The Door*

MAGDA SZABÓ Iza's Ballad*

MAGDA SZABÓ Katalin Street*

ANTAL SZERB Journey by Moonlight*

ELIZABETH TAYLOR Angel*

ELIZABETH TAYLOR A Game of Hide and Seek*

ELIZABETH TAYLOR A View of the Harbour*

ELIZABETH TAYLOR You'll Enjoy It When You Get There: The Stories of Elizabeth Taylor*

TEFFI Memories: From Moscow to the Black Sea*

TEFFI Tolstoy, Rasputin, Others, and Me: The Best of Teffi*

HENRY DAVID THOREAU The Journal: 1837–1861*

ALEKSANDAR TIŠMA The Book of Blam*

ALEKSANDAR TIŠMA The Use of Man*

TATYANA TOLSTAYA The Slynx

TATYANA TOLSTAYA White Walls: Collected Stories

EDWARD JOHN TRELAWNY Records of Shelley, Byron, and the Author

LIONEL TRILLING The Liberal Imagination*

LIONEL TRILLING The Middle of the Journey*

THOMAS TRYON The Other*

MARINA TSVETAEVA Earthly Signs: Moscow Diaries, 1917–1922*

IVAN TURGENEV Virgin Soil

JULES VALLÈS The Child

RAMÓN DEL VALLE-INCLÁN Tyrant Banderas*

MARK VAN DOREN Shakespeare

CARL VAN VECHTEN The Tiger in the House

ELIZABETH VON ARNIM The Enchanted April*

EDWARD LEWIS WALLANT The Tenants of Moonbloom

ROBERT WALSER Berlin Stories*

ROBERT WALSER Girlfriends, Ghosts, and Other Stories*

ROBERT WALSER Jakob von Gunten

ROBERT WALSER A Schoolboy's Diary and Other Stories*

REX WARNER Men and Gods

SYLVIA TOWNSEND WARNER Lolly Willowes*

SYLVIA TOWNSEND WARNER Mr. Fortune*

SYLVIA TOWNSEND WARNER Summer Will Show*

JAKOB WASSERMANN My Marriage*

ALEKSANDER WAT My Century*

C.V. WEDGWOOD The Thirty Years War

SIMONE WEIL On the Abolition of All Political Parties*

SIMONE WEIL AND RACHEL BESPALOFF War and the Iliad

HELEN WEINZWEIG Basic Black with Pearls*

GLENWAY WESCOTT Apartment in Athens*

GLENWAY WESCOTT The Pilgrim Hawk*

REBECCA WEST The Fountain Overflows

EDITH WHARTON The New York Stories of Edith Wharton*

KATHARINE S. WHITE Onward and Upward in the Garden*

PATRICK WHITE Riders in the Chariot

T. H. WHITE The Goshawk*

JOHN WILLIAMS Augustus*

JOHN WILLIAMS Butcher's Crossing*

JOHN WILLIAMS (EDITOR) English Renaissance Poetry: A Collection of Shorter Poems*

JOHN WILLIAMS Stoner*

ANGUS WILSON Anglo-Saxon Attitudes

EDMUND WILSON Memoirs of Hecate County

RUDOLF AND MARGARET WITTKOWER Born Under Saturn

GEOFFREY WOLFF Black Sun*

FRANCIS WYNDHAM The Complete Fiction

JOHN WYNDHAM Chocky

JOHN WYNDHAM The Chrysalids

BÉLA ZOMBORY-MOLDOVÁN The Burning of the World: A Memoir of 1914*

STEFAN ZWEIG Beware of Pity*

STEFAN ZWEIG Chess Story*

STEFAN ZWEIG Confusion*

STEFAN ZWEIG Journey Into the Past*

STEFAN ZWEIG The Post-Office Girl*